First Term
at Malory Towers

This is the first book
in the Malory Towers series

Dragon
Grafton Books
A Division of the Collins Publishing Group
8 Grafton Street, London W1X 3LA

Published by Dragon Books 1967
Reprinted 1970, 1971, 1972, 1973, 1974, 1975,
1976 (twice), 1977, 1978, 1979, 1980 (twice), 1981,
1982 (twice), 1983, 1984 (twice), 1985, 1986 (twice)

First published in Great Britain by
Methuen & Co Ltd 1946

Copyright © Darrell Waters Ltd 1946

ISBN 0-583-30026-X

Printed and bound in Great Britain by
Collins, Glasgow

Set in Times

Enid Blyton

First Term at Malory Towers

DRAGON
GRAFTON BOOKS
A Division of the Collins Publishing Group

LONDON GLASGOW
TORONTO SYDNEY AUCKLAND

Up the steps went Darrell, feeling lost and lonely

Darrell Rivers looked at herself in the glass. It was almost time to start for the train, but there was just a minute to see how she looked in her new school uniform.

"It's jolly nice," said Darrell, turning herself about. "Brown coat, brown hat, orange ribbon, and a brown tunic underneath with an orange belt. I like it."

Her mother looked into Darrell's room, and smiled. "Admiring yourself?" she said. "Well, I like it all too. I must say Malory Towers has a lovely school uniform. Come along, Darrell. We don't want to miss the train your very first term!"

Darrell felt excited. She was going to boarding school for the first time. Malory Towers did not take children younger than twelve, so Darrell would be one of the youngest there. She looked forward to many terms of fun and friendship, work and play.

"What will it be like?" she kept wondering. "I've read lots of school stories, but I expect it won't be quite the same at Malory Towers. Every school is different. I do hope I make some friends there."

Darrell was sad at leaving her own friends behind her. None of them was going to Malory Towers. She had been to a day-school with them, and most of them were either staying on there or going to different boarding schools.

Her trunk was packed full. On the side was painted in big black letters DARRELL RIVERS. On the labels were the letters M.T. for Malory Towers. Darrell had only to carry her tennis racket in its press, and

5

her small bag in which her mother had packed her things for the first night.

"Your trunks won't be unpacked the first evening," she said. "So each girl has to take a small hand-bag with her nighty and tooth-brush and things like that. Here is your ten-shilling note. You must make that last a whole term, because no girl in your form is allowed to have more pocket-money than that."

"I shall make it do!" said Darrell, putting it into her purse. "There won't be much I have to buy at school! There's the taxi waiting, Mother. Let's go!"

She had already said good-bye to her father, who had driven off to his work that morning. He had squeezed her hard and said "Good-bye and good luck, Darrell. You'll get a lot out of Malory Towers, because it's a fine school. Be sure you give them a lot back!"

Now they were off at last, the trunk in the taxi too, beside the driver. Darrell put her head out to take a last look at her home. "I'll be back soon!" she called, to the big black cat who sat on the wall, washing himself. "I'll miss you all at first but I'll soon settle down. Shan't I, Mother?"

"Of course," said her mother. "You'll have a lovely time! You won't want to come home for the summer holidays!"

They had to go up to London to catch the train for Cornwall, where Malory Towers was. "There's a special train always, for Malory Towers," said Mrs. Rivers. "Look, there's a notice up. Malory Towers. Platform 7. Come along. We're in nice time. I'll stay with you a few minutes and see you safely with your house-mistress, and her girls, then I'll go."

They went on to the platform. A long train was drawn up there, labelled Malory Towers. All the carriages were reserved for the girls of that school. The train had different labels stuck in the windows. The first lot said "North Tower." The second lot said

6

"South Tower." Then came compartments labelled "West Tower" and others labelled "East Tower".

"You're North Tower," said her mother. "Malory Towers has four different boarding houses for its girls, all topped by a tower. You'll be in North Tower, the Head Mistress said, and your house-mistress is Miss Potts. We must find her."

Darrell stared about her at the girls on the crowded platform. They all seemed to be Malory girls, for she saw the brown coats and hats, with the orange ribbons, everywhere. They all seemed to know one another, and laughed and chattered at the tops of their voices. Darrell felt suddenly shy.

"I shall never never know all these girls!" she thought, as she stared round. "Gracious, what big ones some of them are! They look quite grown-up. I shall be terrified of them."

Certainly the girls in the top forms seemed very grown-up to Darrell. They took no notice at all of the little ones. The younger girls made way for them, and they climbed into their carriages in a rather lordly manner.

"Hallo, Lottie! Hallo, Mary! I say, there's Penelope! Hie, Penny, come over here. Hilda, you never wrote to me in the hols., you mean pig! Jean, come into our carriage!"

The gay voices sounded all up and down the platform. Darrell looked for her mother. Ah, there she was, talking to a keen-faced mistress. That must be Miss Potts. Darrell stared at her. Yes, she liked her – she liked the way her eyes twinkled – but there was something very determined about her mouth. It wouldn't do to get into her bad books.

Miss Potts came over and smiled down at Darrell. "Well, new girl!" she said. "You'll be in my carriage going down – look, that one over there. The new girls always go with me."

"Oh, are there new girls besides me – in my form, I mean?" asked Darrell.

"Oh, yes. Two more. They haven't arrived yet. Mrs. Rivers, here is a girl in Darrell's form – Alicia Johns. She will look after Darrell for you, when you've said good-bye."

"Hallo," said Alicia, and two bright eyes twinkled at Darrell. "I'm in your form. Do you want to get a corner-seat? If so, you'd better come now."

"Then I'll say good-bye, dear," said Mrs. Rivers, cheerfully, and she kissed Darrell and gave her a hug. "I'll write as soon as I get your letter. Have a lovely time!"

"Yes, I will," said Darrell, and watched her mother go down the platform. She didn't have time to feel lonely because Alicia took complete charge of her at once, pushed her to Miss Pott's carriage, and shoved her up the step. "Put your bag in one corner and I'll put mine opposite," said Alicia. "Then we can stand at the door and see what's happening. I say – look over there. Picture of How Not to Say Good-bye to your Darling Daughter!"

Darrell looked to where Alicia nodded. She saw a girl about her own age, dressed in the same school uniform, but with her hair long and loose down her back. She was clinging to her mother and wailing.

"Now what that mother should do would be to grin, shove some chocolate at her and go!" said Alicia. "If you've got a kid like that, it's hopeless to do anything else. Poor little mother's darling!"

The mother was almost as bad as the girl. Tears were running down her face too. Miss Potts walked firmly up to them.

"Now you watch Potty," said Alicia. Darrell felt rather shocked. Potty! What a name to give your house-mistress. Anyway, Miss Potts didn't look in the least potty. She looked thoroughly all-there.

"I'll take Gwendoline," she said to the girl's mother. "It's time she went to her carriage. She'll soon settle down there, Mrs. Lacey."

Gwendoline appeared ready to go, but her mother clung to her still. Alicia snorted. "See what's made Gwendoline such an idiot?" she said. "Her mother! Well, I'm glad mine is sensible. Yours looked jolly nice too – cheerful and jolly."

Darrell was pleased at this praise of her mother. She watched Miss Potts firmly disentangle Gwendoline from her mother and lead her towards them.

"Alicia! Here's another one," she said, and Alicia pulled Gwendoline up into the carriage.

Gwendoline's mother came to the carriage too and looked in. "Take a corner-seat, darling," she said. "And don't sit with your back to the engine. You know how sick it makes you. And . . ."

Another girl came up to the carriage, a small, sturdy girl, with a plain face and hair tightly plaited back. "Is this Miss Potts's carriage?" she asked.

"Yes," said Alicia. "Are you the third new girl? North Tower?"

"Yes. I'm Sally Hope," said the girl.

"Where's your mother?" asked Alicia. "She ought to go and deliver you to Miss Potts first, so that you can be crossed off her list."

"Oh, Mother didn't bother to come up with me," said Sally. "I came by myself."

"Gracious!" said Alicia. "Well, mothers are all different. Some come along and smile and say goodbye, and some come along and weep and wail – and some just don't come at all."

"Alicia – don't talk so much," came Miss Potts's voice. She knew Alicia's wild tongue. Mrs. Lacey suddenly looked annoyed, and forgot to give any more instructions to Gwendoline. She stared at Alicia angrily.

Fortunately the guard blew his whistle just then and there was a wild scramble for seats.

Miss Potts jumped in with two or three more girls. The door slammed. Gwendoline's mother peered in, but alas, Gwendoline was on the floor, hunting for something she had dropped.

"Where's Gwendoline?" came Mrs. Lacey's voice. "I must say good-bye. Where's . . ."

But the train was now puffing out. Gwendoline sat up and howled.

"I didn't say good-bye!" she wailed.

"Well, how many times did you want to?" demanded Alicia. "You'd already said it about twenty times."

Miss Potts looked at Gwendoline. She had already sized her up and knew her to be a spoilt, only child, selfish, and difficult to handle at first.

She looked at quiet little Sally Hope. Funny little girl, with her tight plaits and prim, closed-up face. No mother had come to see her off. Did Sally care? Miss Potts couldn't tell.

Then she looked at Darrell. It was quite easy to read Darrell. She never hid anything, and she said what she thought, though not so bluntly as Alicia did.

"A nice, straightforward, trustable girl," thought Miss Potts. "Can be a bit of a monkey, I should think. She looks as if she has good brains. I'll see that she uses them! I can do with a girl like Darrell in North Tower!"

The girls began to talk. "What's Malory Towers like?" asked Darrell. "I've seen a photograph of it, of course. It looked awfully big."

"It is. It's got the most gorgeous view over the sea, too," said Alicia. "It's built on the cliff, you know. It's lucky you're in North Tower – that's got the best view of all!"

"Does each Tower have its own schoolrooms?" asked Darrell. Alicia shook her head.

"Oh, no! All the girls from each of the four Tower

houses go to the same classrooms. There are about sixty girls in each house. Pamela is head of ours. There she is over there!"

Pamela was a tall, quiet girl, who had got into the carriage with another girl about her own age. They seemed very friendly with Miss Potts, and were eagerly discussing with her the happenings planned for the term.

Alicia, another girl called Tessie, Sally and Darrell chattered too. Gwendoline sat in her corner and looked gloomy. Nobody paid her any attention at all, and she wasn't used to that!

She gave a little sob, and looked at the others out of the corner of her eye. Sharp Alicia saw the look and grinned. "Just putting it on!" she whispered to Darrell. "People who really do feel miserable always turn away and hide it somehow. Don't take any notice of our darling Gwendoline."

Poor Gwendoline! If she had only known it, Alicia's lack of sympathy was the best thing for her. She had always had far too much of it, and life at Malory Towers was not going to be easy for her.

"Cheer up, Gwendoline," said Miss Potts, in a cheerful tone, and immediately turned to talk to the big girls again.

"I feel sick," announced Gwendoline at last, quite determined to be in the limelight and get sympathy somehow.

"You don't look it," said the downright Alicia. "Does she, Miss Potts? I always go green when I feel sick."

Gwendoline wished she could really be sick! That would serve this sharp-tongued girl right. She leaned back against the back of the seat, and murmured faintly. "I really do feel sick! Oh, dear, what shall I do?"

"Here, wait a bit – I've got a paper bag," said Alicia, and fished a big one out of her bag. "I've got a brother who's always sick in a car, so Mother takes paper bags with her wherever she goes, for Sam. I always think it's funny to see him stick his nose in it, poor Sam – like a horse with a nose-bag!"

Nobody could help laughing at Alicia's story. Gwendoline didn't, of course, but looked angry. That horrid girl, poking fun at her again. She wasn't going to like her at all.

After that Gwendoline sat quiet, and made no further attempt to get the attention of the others. She was afraid of what Alicia might say next.

But Darrell looked at Alicia with amusement and liking. How she would like her for a friend! What fun they could have together!

Malory Towers

It was a long journey to Malory Towers, but as there was a dining-car on the train, and the girls took it in turns to go and have their midday meal, that made a good break. They had tea on the train too. At first all the girls were gay and chattery, but as the day wore on they fell silent. Some of them slept. It was such a long journey!

It was exciting to reach the station for Malory Towers. The school lay a mile or two away, and there were big motor coaches standing outside the station to take the girls to the school.

"Come on," said Alicia, clutching hold of Darrell's arm. "If we're quick we can get one of the front seats in a coach, beside the driver. Hurry! Got your bag?"

"I'll come too," said Gwendoline. But the others were gone long before she had collected her belongings. They climbed up into front seats. The other girls came out in twos and threes, and the station's one and only porter helped the drivers to load the many trunks on to the coaches.

"Can we see Malory Towers from here?" asked Darrell, looking all round.

"No. I'll tell you when we can. There's a corner where we suddenly get a glimpse of it," said Alicia.

"Yes. It's lovely to get that sudden view of it," said Pamela, the quiet head-girl of North Tower, who had got into the coach just behind Alicia and Darrell. Her eyes shone as she spoke. "I think Malory Towers shows at its best when we come to that corner, especially if the sun is behind it."

Darrell could feel the warmth in Pamela's voice as she spoke of the school she loved. She looked at her and liked her.

Pamela saw her look and laughed. "You're lucky, Darrell," she said. "You're just beginning at Malory Towers! You've got terms and terms before you. I'm just ending. Another term or two, and I shan't be coming to Malory Towers any more – except as an old girl. You make the most of it while you can."

"I shall," said Darrell, and stared ahead, waiting for her first glimpse of the school she was to go to for at least six years.

They rounded a corner. Alicia nudged her arm. "There you are, look! Over there, on that hill! The sea is behind, far down the cliff, but you can't see that, of course."

Darrell looked. She saw a big, square-looking building of soft grey stone standing high up on a hill. The hill was really a cliff, that fell steeply down to the sea. At each end of the gracious building stood rounded towers. Darrell could glimpse two other towers behind as well, making four in all. North Tower, South, East and West.

The windows shone. The green creeper that covered

13

parts of the wall climbed almost to the roof in places. It looked like an old-time castle.

"My school," thought Darrell, and a little warm feeling came into her heart. "It's fine. How lucky I am to be having Malory Towers as my school-home for so many years. I shall love it."

"Do you like it?" asked Alicia, impatiently.

"Yes. Very much," said Darrell. "But I shall never never know my way about it! It's so big."

"Oh, I'll soon show you," said Alicia. "It's surprising how quickly you get to know your way round."

The coach turned another corner and Malory Towers was lost to sight. It came into view again, nearer still, round the next corner, and it wasn't very long before all the coaches roared up to the flight of steps that led to the great front door.

'It's just like a castle entrance!" said Darrell.

"Yes," said Gwendoline, unexpectedly, from behind them. "I shall feel like a fairy princess, going up those steps!" She tossed her loose golden hair back over her shoulders.

"You would!" said Alicia, scornfully. "But you'll soon get ideas like that out of your head when Potty gets going on you."

Darrell got down and was immediately lost in a crowd of girls, all swarming up the steps. She looked round for Alicia, but she seemed to have disappeared. So up the steps went Darrell, clutching her small bag and racket, feeling rather lost and lonely in the chattering crowd of girls. She felt in quite a panic without the friendly Alicia!

After that things were rather a blur. Darrell didn't know where to go and she didn't know what to do. She looked vainly for Alicia, or Pamela, the head-girl. Was she supposed to go straight to North Tower? Everyone seemed to know exactly what to do and where to go, except poor Darrell!

14

Then she saw Miss Potts, and felt a wave of relief. She went up to her, and Miss Potts looked down, smiling. "Hallo! Feeling lost? Where's that rascal of an Alicia? She ought to look after you. All North Tower girls are to go there and unpack their night-bags. Matron is waiting for you all."

Darrell had no idea which way to go for North Tower, so she stood by Miss Potts, waiting. Alicia soon reappeared again, accompanied by a crowd of girls.

"Hallo!" she said to Darrell. "I lost you. These are all girls in our form, but I won't tell you their names just now. You'll only get muddled. Some are North Tower girls, but some belong to the other houses. Come on, let's go to North Tower and see Matron. Where's darling Gwendoline?"

"Alicia," said Miss Potts, her voice stern, but her eyes twinkling. "Give Gwendoline a chance!"

"And Sally Hope? Where's she?" said Alicia. "Come on, Sally. All right, Miss Potts, I'll take them along to North Tower, and nurse them a bit!"

Sally, Gwendoline and Darrell followed Alicia. They were in a big hall, that had doors leading off on either side, and a wide staircase curving upwards.

"The assembly hall, the gyms., the lab., the art-rooms, and the needlework room are all on this side," said Alicia. "Come on, we'll cross the Court to get to our tower."

Darrell wondered what the Court was. She soon found out. Malory Towers was built round a large oblong space, called the Court. Alicia took her and the others out of a door opposite the entrance they had come in by, and there lay the Court surrounded on all sides by the buildings.

"What a lovely place!" said Darrell. "What's that sunk piece in the middle?"

She pointed to a great circle of green grass sunk a good way below the level of the Court. Round the

15

sloping sides of the circle were stone seats. It looked like an open-air circus ring, the ring sunk low, and the stone seats rising upwards around it, Darrell thought.

"That's where we act plays in the summer," said Alicia. "The players perform in the ring, and the audience sit round on those stone seats. We have good fun."

Round the sunk circle, on the level, was a beautifully set out garden, with roses and all kinds of flowers planted there. Green lawns, not yet cut by the gardeners, were set between the beds.

"It's warm and sheltered in the Court," said Darrell.

"It's too hot in the summer," said Alicia, steering them all across the Court to the opposite side. "But you should see it in the Easter term! When we come back, in January, leaving our own homes in frost and maybe snow, we find snowdrops and aconites and primroses blooming in all the beds here, in the sheltered Court. It's gorgeous. Well, look at the tulips coming out here already, and it's only April!"

At each end of the hollow oblong of buildings was a tower. Alicia was making for North Tower. It was exactly like the other three. Darrell looked at it. It was four storeys high. Alicia stopped short just outside.

"On the ground floor there's our dining-hall, our common rooms, where we go when we're not in class, and the kitchens. On the second floor are the dormies, where we sleep – dormitories, you know. On the third floor are more dormies. On the top floor are the bedrooms of the staff, and the box rooms for our luggage."

"And each house is the same, I suppose?" said Darrell, and she looked up at her tower. "I wish I slept right at the top there, in the tower itself. What a lovely view I'd have!"

Girls were going in and out of the open door at the bottom of North Tower. "Buck up!" they called to

Alicia. "Supper's in a few minutes' time – something good by the smell of it!"

"We always get a jolly good supper the day we arrive," said Alicia. "After that – not so good! Cocoa and biscuits, something like that. Come on, let's find Matron."

Each of the Tower houses had its own matron, responsible for the girls' health and well-being. The matron of North Tower was a plump, bustling woman, dressed in starched apron and print frock, very neat and spotless.

Alicia took the new girls to her. "Three more for you to dose and scold and run after!" said Alicia, with a grin.

Darrell looked at Matron, frowning over the long lists in her hand. Her hair was neatly tucked under a pretty cap, tied in a bow under her chin. She looked so spotless that Darrell began to feel very dirty and untidy. She felt a little scared of Matron, and hoped she wouldn't make her take nasty medicine too often.

Then Matron looked up and smiled, and at once Darrell's fears fell away. She couldn't be afraid of a person who smiled like that, with her eyes and her mouth and even her nose too!

"Now let me see – you're Darrell Rivers," said Matron, ticking off her name on a list. "Got your health certificate with you? Give it to me, please. And you're Sally Hope."

"No, I'm Gwendoline Mary Lacey," said Gwendoline.

"And don't forget the Mary," said Alicia, pertly. "Dear Gwendoline Mary."

"That's enough, Alicia," said Matron, ticking away down her list. "You're as bad as your mother used to be. No, worse, I think."

Alicia grinned. "Mother came to Malory Towers when she was a girl," she told the others. "She was in

17

North Tower too, and Matron had her for years. She sent you her best love, Matron. She says she wishes she could send all my brothers to you too. She's sure you're the only person who can manage them."

"If they're anything like you, I'm very glad they're not here," said Matron. "One of the Johns family at a time is quite enough for me. Your mother put some grey hairs into my head, and you've certainly done your bit in adding a few more."

She smiled again. She had a wise, kindly face, and any girl who fell ill felt safe in Matron's care. But woe betide any pretender, or any lazy girl or careless one! Then Matron's smile snapped off, her face closed up, and her eyes glinted dangerously!

A big gong boomed through North Tower. "Supper," said Matron. "Unpack your things afterwards, Alicia. Your train was late and you must all be very tired. All first-formers are to go to bed immediately after supper tonight.'

"Oh, *Ma*tron!" began Alicia, groaning. "Can't we just have ten minutes after . . ."

"I said *immediately*, Alicia," said Matron. "Go along now. Wash your hands quickly and go down. Hurry!"

And in five minutes' time Alicia and the others were sitting down, enjoying a good supper. They were hungry. Darrell looked round at the tables. She was sure she would never know all the girls in her house! And she was sure she would never dare to join in their laugh and chatter either.

But she would, of course – and very soon too!

After supper, obeying Matron's command, all the first-formers went up to their dormitory. Darrell was delighted with the room. It was long, and had windows all down the length of it, which, to Darrell's joy, overlooked the sea. She stood there, hearing the faraway sound of waves on the beach, watching the slowly moving blue sea. What a lovely place this was!

"Buck up, Dreamy!" said Alicia's voice. "Matron will be along in two ticks."

Darrell turned. She looked at the room. It had ten beds in it, each divided from the next by a white curtain which could be drawn or pulled back as the girls wished.

Each girl had a white bed with a coloured eiderdown. The eiderdowns were different colours and made a pretty show as Darrell looked down the row of beds. In each cubicle there was a cupboard to hang things, and a chest of drawers with a mirror on top. There were wash-basins with hot and cold water at each end of the room.

The girls were busy unpacking their small bags. Darrell opened hers. She shook out her night-dress. She took her face-flannel, her tooth-brush and paste. A clean towel hung ready for her on a rail at the side of her chest of drawers.

"It will be fun to sleep here, with all the others," thought Darrell. "What fun we shall have talking at night. We could have dormy games too, I should think."

All the first-formers were in the same dormy. Alicia was there, Darrell, Sally and Gwendoline. There were six other girls besides. They stared at the three new girls as they ran to and from the wash-basins, washing, and cleaning their teeth.

One of the girls looked at her watch. "Get into bed, everyone!" she ordered. She was a tall, dark girl, quiet in her manner. Everyone but Gwendoline scrambled into bed. Gwendoline was still brushing out her fine golden hair. She was counting as she brushed it.

"Fifty-four, fifty-five, fifty-six . . ."

"Hey, you new girl – what's your name – get into bed!" ordered the tall dark girl again.

"I've got to brush my hair a hundred times each night," protested Gwendoline. "Now I've forgotten what number I got to!"

"Shut up and get into bed, Gwendoline Mary," said Alicia, who was next to Gwendoline. "Katherine is the head of our dormy. You've got to do what she says."

"But I promised M-M-Mo . . ." began Gwendoline, tears welling up. "I promised Mother to b-b-b-brush my hair a hundred times each night!"

"You can add the number of brushings you leave out tonight on to tomorrow night," came the head-girl's cool voice. "Get into bed, please."

"Oh, just let me finish!" said Gwendoline and began frantically brushing again. "Fifty-seven, fifty . . ."

"Shall I spank her with my brush, Katherine?" said Alicia, sitting up. Gwendoline gave a squeal and leapt into bed. The girls laughed. They all knew that Alicia had no intention of spanking Gwendoline.

Gwendoline lay down, angry. She determined to make herself miserable and cry. She thought of her mother, and her faraway home, and she began to sniff.

"Do blow your nose, Gwendoline," said Alicia, sleepily.

"Stop talking," said Katherine. There was silence in the room. Sally Hope gave a little sigh. Darrell wondered if she was asleep. The curtains between her bed and Sally's were pulled back. No, Sally was not asleep.

20

She lay with her eyes wide open. There was no tears in them, but her face looked sad.

"Perhaps she's homesick," thought Darrell, and thought of her home too. But she was too sensible to be silly about it, and too excited to be at Malory Towers to miss her home. After all, she had badly wanted to come, and here she was – and she meant to be very happy and have a lot of fun.

Matron arrived. She took a look down the beds. One or two of the girls were already fast asleep, tired out. Matron walked down the long room, twitched an eider-down into place, turned off a dripping tap, and pulled the curtains across the windows, for it was still very light outside.

"Good night," she said, in a low voice. "And no talking, please!"

"Good night, Matron," murmured those girls who were not yet asleep. Darrell peeped to see if Matron's nice smile was on her face. She caught sight of Darrell's peeping eyes and nodded, smiling. "Sleep well!" she said, and went out quietly.

Gwendoline was the only one who tried to keep awake. What had Mother said to her? "You'll feel dreadful tonight, I know, darling, but be brave, won't you?"

So Gwendoline was determined to lie awake and feel dreadful. But her eyes wouldn't keep open! They shut and soon Gwendoline was as fast asleep as the others. And at home her mother was dabbing her eyes, and saying "Poor little Gwen! I shouldn't have sent her away from me! I feel she's awake and crying her heart out!"

But Gwendoline was giving little contented snores, dreaming happily of how she would queen it over the girls here, be top of her form, and best at all games.

A loud bell awoke all the girls the next morning. At first Darrell couldn't imagine where she was. Then she heard Alicia's voice. "Get up, lazy-bones! You've got to make your bed before breakfast!"

Darrell leapt out of bed. The sun poured into the room, for Katherine had drawn the curtains back. A loud chattering began. Girls hopped across the room to the washbasins. Darrell dressed quickly, proud to put on her brown tunic with its brown orange belt, just like all the other girls wore. She brushed her hair back and put in two slides to keep it tidy. Gwendoline left her hair loose over her shoulders.

"You can't have it like that," said Alicia. "Not in *school*, Gwendoline!"

"I've always had it like this," said Gwendoline, an obstinate look coming over her pretty, silly little face.

"Well, it looks awful," said Alicia.

"It does not!" said Gwendoline. "You only say that because your hair is short and coarse."

Alicia winked at Katherine, who was coming up. "Better let dear Gwendoline show off her long, fine-as-silk hair, don't you think so?" she said, in a bland voice. "Miss Potts might be delighted to see it like that."

"My governess, Miss Winter, always liked it like this," said Gwendoline, looking pleased.

"Oh – haven't you been to a school before? Have you just had a governess?" asked Alicia. "That explains a lot."

"What does it explain?" asked Gwendoline, haughtily.

"Never mind. You'll find out," said Alicia. "Ready, Darrell? That's the breakfast gong. Tuck your sheet in well. That's right, Gwendoline, fold up your nighty. Look at Sally – there's a new girl for you! Everything done to time, nobody's got to chivvy her round!"

Sally gave a little smile. She hardly said a word. She did not seem in the least shy, but she was so quiet and self-possessed that Darrell could hardly believe she was a new girl. She always seemed to know exactly what to do.

They all went down to the dining-hall. The long tables were ready, and girls were already seating themselves, greeting their house-mistress politely. Matron was there too, and a third grown-up, whom Darrell had not seen before.

"That's Mam'zelle Dupont," whispered Alicia. "We've got two French mistresses at Malory Towers. One's fat and jolly and the other's thin and sour. We've got the fat and jolly one this term. They've both got simply awful tempers, so I hope you're pretty good at French."

"Well, no, I'm not really," said Darrell, wishing she was.

"Mam'zelle Dupont hates Mam'zelle Rougier and Mam'zelle Rougier hates Mam'zelle Dupont," went on Alicia. "You should see the fur fly sometimes. Matron has to be sent for to calm them down when they get too bad!"

Darrell's eyes opened wide. Katherine, across the table, laughed. "Don't believe all that Alicia says," she said. "Her tongue runs away with her sometimes. Nobody has ever seen our two Mam'zelles fly at each other's throats yet."

"Ah, but they will one day – and I hope I'll be there to see it," said Alicia.

Mam'zelle Dupont was short, fat and round. She wore her hair in a little bun on top. Her eyes, black and beady, were never still. She wore a black frock that fitted her perfectly, and well-fitting black shoes on her tiny feet.

She was short-sighted but she would not wear glasses. She had instead a pair of long-handled glasses, called lorgnettes, which she wore dangling on a long black ribbon. These she used when she wanted to see anything at close quarters, holding them to her eyes with her hand.

Alicia, who was a good mimic, could keep her class in fits of laughter, blinking like poor Mam'zelle, and holding imaginary glasses up to her nose. But she was just as much in awe of Mam'zelle Dupont as anyone else, and did not rouse her hot temper if she could help it.

"New girls must go to see the Head Mistress after breakfast," announced Miss Potts. "There are three in the first form, two in the second form, and one in the fourth. You can all go together. Join us in the assembly room for Prayers later. Pamela, will you take the new girls to the Head, please?"

Pamela, head-girl of North Tower House, rose. The new girls stood up, Darrell among them. They followed Pamela. She took them out of the door that let into the Court, and then in through another door set in the building that ran between East and North Tower. The Head Mistress's rooms were there, and so was the San. or sanatorium, where any sick girl went.

They came to a door painted a deep cream colour. Pamela knocked. A low voice said "Come in!"

Pamela opened the door. "I've brought the new girls to you, Miss Grayling," she said.

"Thank you, Pamela," said the low voice again, and Darrell saw a grey-haired woman sitting at a desk, writing. She had a calm, unwrinkled face, eyes that were startlingly blue, and a very firm mouth. Darrell felt frightened of this calm, low-voiced Head Mistress, and hoped she would never have to be sent to her for misbehaviour!

The new girls stood in a row before the Head, and Miss Grayling looked at them all closely. Darrell felt herself going red, she couldn't imagine why. Her knees felt a bit wobbly too. She hoped Miss Grayling wouldn't ask her any questions, for she was sure she wouldn't be able to say a word!

Miss Grayling asked them their names, and spoke a few words to each girl. Then she addressed them all solemnly.

"One day you will leave school and go out into the world as young women. You should take with you eager minds, kind hearts, and a will to help. You should take with you a good understanding of many things, and a willingness to accept responsibility and show yourselves as women to be loved and trusted. All these things you will be able to learn at Malory Towers – if you *will*. I do not count as our successes those who have won scholarships and passed exams., though these are good things to do. I count as our successes those who learn to be good-hearted and kind, sensible and trustable, good, sound women the world can lean on. Our failures are those who do not learn these things in the years they are here."

These words were spoken so gravely and solemnly that Darrell hardly breathed. She immediately longed to be one of Malory Towers' successes.

"It is easy for some of you to learn these things, and hard for others. But easy or hard, they must be learnt if you are to be happy, after you leave here, and if you are to bring happiness to others."

There was a pause. Then Miss Grayling spoke again, in a lighter tone. "You will all get a tremendous lot out of your time at Malory Towers. See that you give a lot back!"

"Oh!" said Darrell, surprised and pleased, quite forgetting that she had thought she wouldn't be able to speak a word, "that's *exactly* what my father said to me when he said good-bye, Miss Grayling!"

"Did he?" said Miss Grayling, looking with smiling eyes at the eager little girl. "Well, as you have parents who think in that way, I imagine you will be one of the lucky ones, and will find that the things I have been speaking of will be easy to learn. Perhaps one day Malory Towers will be proud of you."

A few more words and the girls were told to go. Very much impressed they walked out of the room. Not even Gwendoline said a word. Whatever they might do, in the years to come at Malory Towers, each girl wanted, at that moment, to do her best. Whether or not that wish would last, depended on the girl.

Then they went to the Assembly Hall for Prayers, found their places, and waited for Miss Grayling to come to the platform.

Soon the words of a hymn sounded in the big hall. The first day of term had begun. Darrell sang with all her might, happy and excited. What a lot she would have to tell her mother when she wrote!

Miss Potts' Form

All the school met each morning for prayers. The girls stood together in their classes – first-formers of North Tower, South, East, and West Tower, all together, and so on.

Darrell took a nervous look at her class. What a big one it seemed! About twenty-five or thirty girls, surely. Miss Potts, her house-mistress, was also the first-form mistress. There was Mam'zelle Dupont, singing lustily, and the teacher beside her must be the other French mistress. But how different! She was skinny, tall and bony. Her hair too was done up in a little bun, but at the back instead of on top. Darrell thought she looked bad-tempered.

Alicia told her which the other mistresses were "That's the history mistress, Miss Carton over there – see her – the one with the high collar and pince-nez

26

glasses on her nose. She's frightfully clever, and awfully sarcastic if you don't like history. And that's the art mistress, Miss Linnie – she's awfully nice. Very easy-going."

Darrell hoped she would have a lot to do with Miss Linnie, if she was easy-going. She looked nice. She was young and had red hair done in little curls.

"That's the music-master – Mr. Young – see him? He's always either in a very good temper or a very bad one. We always try and find out which, when he takes us for music or singing."

The matrons of the four houses were at Prayers too. Darrell saw her own Matron, looking a little stern, as she always did when she was thinking hard of what she was doing. Alicia began whispering again.

"And that's . . ."

Miss Potts's eye swung round to her, and Alicia immediately stopped whispering and studied her hymn-book. Miss Potts did not look kindly on people who whispered at any time, least of all in Prayers.

Prayers over, the girls filed off to their various class-rooms. These ran all along the west side of Malory Towers, and soon that building was filled with the sound of hurrying feet, laughter and chattering. There was no rule about silence in the corridors in the part of the building where the classrooms were.

The first-formers filed into their own classroom, a room with a lovely view over the sea. It was a big room, with the mistress's desk at one end, and cupboards at the other. Desks and chairs were arranged in orderly rows.

"Bags I one by the window!" said a fat girl and plumped herself down there.

"Bags I one too," said Gwendoline. But the fat girl stared in surprise.

"You're new aren't you? Well, you can't choose your own seat, then. New girls have to take the desks left over when the old girls have chosen the ones they want."

Gwendoline went red. She tossed her golden hair back over her shoulders and looked sulky.

She stood close by the desk she had chosen, not quite daring to take it, but too obstinate to leave it. A small wiry girl pushed her away.

"Bags I this desk! Hallo, Rita! Did you have nice hols.? Awful to be back with old Potty, isn't it?"

Darrell stood and waited till she saw that all the girls except herself, Sally and Gwendoline and one or two others, had desks. Then she slipped into one beside Alicia, glad of her good luck. Alicia was exchanging news with a girl on the other side of her. She seemed to be very friendly indeed with her.

She turned to Darrell. "Darrell, this is my friend, Betty Hill. We always sit next to each other. But Betty is in West House, worse luck."

Darrell smiled at Betty, who was a lively-looking girl, with wicked brown eyes and hair that fell over her forehead. She liked Betty but she was sorry to hear that Alicia had a friend already. She had rather hoped that Alicia would be *her* friend. She didn't particularly want either Sally or Gwendoline.

"Sh!" said the girl at the door. "Here comes Potty!"

There was silence at once. The girls stood up, and looked straight before them as they heard the quick, light steps of their form-mistress coming down the corridor outside. She swept into the room, nodded to the girls and said, "You can sit!"

They sat down and waited in silence. Miss Potts took out her list of names and checked them all, tracking down a few more new girls in the other houses. Then she turned to the expectant faces before her.

"Well!" she said, "the summer term is always the best of the lot, with swimming and tennis, picnics and rambles. But please don't make the mistake of thinking

28

that the summer term is nothing *but* a picnic. It isn't. It's good hard work too. Some of you are taking exams. next term. Well, work hard this term, and you'll find the exams. easy next term. But slack this term, and I promise you I shall hear some groans and grumbles *next* term!"

She paused. Then she looked hard at two or three girls. "Last term there were one or two girls who seemed to like to be bottom every week," she said. "Leave that place to the new girls, please, and go up a few places! I never expect much of new girls their first term – but I *shall* expect quite a lot of you."

A few girls went red. Miss Potts went on talking. "I don't really think I've any brainless girls this term," she said, "though I don't know much about the new girls, of course. If you are brainless and near the bottom, we shan't blame you, of course – but if you've got good brains and are down at the bottom, I shall have a lot to say. And you know what *that* means, don't you?"

"Yes," answered most of the girls, fervently. Miss Potts smiled, and her keen face lit up for a moment. "Well, now, after all those threats, let's get on. Here's a list of things each girl must have. If anyone lacks any of them, she must go to Katherine, head-girl of the form, and get them from her at the end of the lesson. I will give ten minutes for that."

Soon a lesson was in full swing. It was maths., and Miss Potts was giving a quick test-paper to see what standard the new girls were up to, and whether the whole form could work together or not. Darrell found the paper quite easy, but Gwendoline groaned and grunted terribly, her golden hair all over the desk.

"What's the matter, Gwendoline?" inquired Miss Potts, unsympathetically.

"Well, my governess, Miss Winter, never showed me how to do sums like this," wailed Gwendoline.

"She put them down quite differently."

"You'll have to learn *my* way now," said Miss Potts. "And Gwendoline – why haven't you done your hair this morning?"

"I *did*," said Gwendoline, raising her big pale blue eyes. "I brushed it well. I gave it forty . . ."

"All right, I don't want details," said Miss Potts. "You can't come to class with it like that. Plait it after Break."

"*Plait* it!" mourned poor Gwendoline, whilst the rest of the class began to giggle. "But I've never . . ."

"That's enough," said Miss Potts. "If you can't plait it and keep it tidy, perhaps your mother could have it cut short next holidays."

Gwendoline looked so horrified that it was all Darrell could do to keep from laughing out loud.

"I told you so!" whispered Alicia, as soon as Miss Potts turned to write something on the blackboard. Gwendoline glared angrily at her and made a face. As if Mother would *dream* of cutting off her beautiful fine sheet of hair. And now to think she'd got to plait it. Why, she didn't even know *how* to plait! Gwendoline was so lost in sulky thought that she hardly answered any of the maths. questions.

The morning went on. Break came and the girls rushed out to play where they liked. Some went for a quick game on one of the many tennis-courts. Some went for a ramble in the grounds. Others lay about in the Court, talking. Darrell would have liked to go with Alicia, but she was with Betty, and Darrell felt sure they wouldn't want a third person. She looked at the other new girls. Two of them, whom she didn't know, had made friends already. Another girl, who had a cousin in the same form, went off with her. Gwendoline was not to be seen. Perhaps she had gone to plait her hair!

Sally Hope was sitting on the grass alone, no expres-

30

sion at all on her closed-up face. Darrell went over to her. "What do you think of Malory Towers?" she said. "I think it's fine."

Sally looked up primly. "It's not bad," she said.

"Were you sorry to leave your other school?" asked Darrell. "I wanted to come to Malory, of course, but I hated leaving all my friends. Didn't you hate leaving all your friends too?"

"I don't think I had any, really," said Sally, considering. Darrell thought that was queer. It was hard to get anything out of Sally. She was polite and answered questions, but she didn't ask any in return.

"Well, I hope I don't have to make *her* my friend!" thought Darrell, at last. "Gracious, here's Gwendoline! *Does* she think she's plaited her hair? It's all undone already!"

"Is my hair all right?" said Gwendoline, in a plaintive voice. "I've tried and tried to plait it. It was beastly of Miss Potts not to let me wear it as I've always worn it. I don't like her."

"Let *me* plait it for you," said Darrell, jumping up. "It doesn't look to me as if you know *how* to plait, Gwendoline!"

She plaited the golden hair deftly and quickly into long braids and tied the ends with bits of narrow ribbon.

"There!" she said, swinging Gwendoline round to look at her. "You look *much* nicer!"

Gwendoline scowled, and forgot to thank Darrell for her help. Actually, she did look much nicer now. "How spoilt she is!" thought Darrell. "Well, little as I want Sally for a friend, I want Gwendoline even less. I should want to slap her for all her silly airs and graces!"

The bell went, and scores of girls raced in to their classrooms. Darrell raced too. She knew where her classroom was. She knew the names of a lot of her form. She would soon be quite at home at Malory Towers!

31

Darrell soon began to settle down. She learnt the names not only of the girls in her form at North Tower, but of every girl there, from the head-girl Pamela, down to Mary-Lou, the youngest but one in the first form. Darrell herself was the youngest girl in North Tower, she found, but she felt that Mary-Lou was very much younger.

Mary-Lou was a scared mouse of a girl. She was frightened of mice, beetles, thunderstorms, noises at night, the dark, and a hundred other things. Poor Mary-Lou, no wonder she had big scared eyes. Darrell, not easily scared of anything, laughed when she saw poor Mary-Lou rush to the other side of the dormy because she saw an earwig on the floor.

There were ten girls in the first-form dormy at North Tower. Katherine, the quiet head-girl. Alicia, the talkative, unruly-tongued monkey. The three new girls, Darrell, Gwendoline, and Sally. Mary-Lou, with her big scared eyes, always ready to shy back like a nervous horse, at anything unexpected.

Then there was clever Irene, a marvel at maths. and music, usually top of the form – but oh, how stupid in the ordinary things of life. If anyone lost her book it was Irene. If anyone went to the wrong classroom at the wrong time it was Irene. It was said that once she had gone to the art-room, thinking that a painting lesson was to be taken there, and had actually sat there for half an hour, apparently waiting for Miss Linnie to come. What she thought had happened to the rest of the class, no one knew.

"But *how* could you sit there all that time and not even *wonder* why nobody came!" said Katherine, in amazement. "What were you thinking of, Irene?"

"I was just thinking of a maths. problem that Potty set us, that's all," said Irene, her eyes shining through her big glasses. "It was rather an interesting one, and there were two or three ways of getting it right. You see . . ."

"Oh, spare us maths. out of school!" groaned Alicia. "Irene, I think you're bats!"

But Irene wasn't. She was a most intelligent girl, who, because her mind was always so deeply at work at something, seemed to forget the smaller, everyday things of life. She had a sense of fun too, and when she was really tickled she came out with a tremendous explosive giggle that startled the class and made Miss Potts jump. It was Alicia's delight to provoke this explosion sometimes, and upset the class.

The other three girls in the form were Jean, a jolly, shrewd girl from Scotland, very able at handling money for various school societies and charities; Emily, a quiet studious girl, clever with her needle, and one of Mam'zelle's favourites because of this; and Violet, a shy, colourless child, very much left out of things because she never seemed to take any interest in them. Half the form never even noticed whether Violet was with them or not.

That made up the ten girls. Darrell felt that she had known them for years after she had lived with them only a few days. She knew the way Irene's stockings always fell down in wrinkles. She knew the way Jean spoke, clipped and sharp, in her Scots accent. She knew that Mam'zelle disliked Jean because Jean was scornful of Mam'zelle's enthusiasms and emotions. Jean herself never went into ecstasies about anything.

Darrell knew Gwendoline's sighs and moans over everything, and Mary-Lou's scared exclamations of fear at any insect or reptile. She liked Katherine's low, firm voice, and air of being able to cope with anything. She knew a great deal about Alicia, but then, so did everyone, for Alicia poured out everything that came into her head, she chattered about her brothers, her mother and father, her dogs, her work, her play, her knitting, her opinion of everything and everybody under the sun.

Alicia had no time at all for airs and graces, pretences, sighs, moans or affectations. She was as downright as Darrell, but not so kind. She was scornful and biting when it pleased her, so that girls like Gwendoline hated her, and those like scared Mary-Lou feared her. Darrell liked her immensely.

"She's so lively," she thought to herself. "Nobody could be dull with Alicia. I wish I was as interesting as she is. Everyone listens when Alicia speaks, even when she says something unkind. But nobody pays much attention when I want to say something. I do really like Alicia, and I wish she hadn't got Betty for a friend. She's just the one I would have chosen."

It took Darrell longer to know the first-formers who came from the other Towers. She saw them in class, but not in the common room or dormies, for the first-formers of the other Towers had their own rooms, of course, in their own Towers. Still, it was enough to know her own Tower girls for a start, Darrell thought.

She didn't know very much about the older girls in her Tower, for she didn't even meet them in the classroom. She saw them at Prayers in the morning, sometimes during the singing-lesson, when Mr. Young took more than one class at a time, and sometimes on the tennis-courts and in the swimming-pool.

She heard a few things about some of them, of course, Marilyn, sixth-former, was captain of the games, and most of the girls liked her immensely. "She's fair and really takes a lot of trouble to coach even the first-formers," said Alicia. "She's as good as old Remmington, the games-mistress, any day. *She* won't bother with the duds, but Marilyn *does*."

34

Everyone appeared to look up to Pamela, the head-girl, too. She was clever, and rather literary. It was said that she was already writing a book. This impressed the first-formers very much. It was hard enough to write a decent composition, let alone a book.

No one seemed to like two girls called Doris and Fanny. "Too spiteful for words," said Alicia, who, of course, could always give an opinion immediately about anyone or anything, from Winston Churchill down to the little boy belonging to the Tower House cook. "They're frightfully pi."

"What do you mean – pi?" said Gwendoline, who hadn't apparently heard that word before.

"Golly – what an ignoramus you are!" said Alicia. "Pi means pious. Religious in the wrong way. Thinking they're wonderful and nobody else is. Trying to stop people's pleasure. They're a sickening pair. Always on the prowl and on the snoop. Once, when I slipped across the Court in the middle of the night to join Betty Hill, in West Tower for a midnight feast, Doris saw me out of the window, and lay in wait for me to come back. Beast."

"Did she catch you?" asked Mary-Lou, her eyes wide with alarm.

" 'Course she didn't! You don't think I'd let myself be caught by the Pi Sisters, do you?" said Alicia, scornfully. "I spotted her when I came back, and shut her in the boot-cupboard."

Irene gave one of her loud explosive giggles and made them all jump. "I'd never think of the things *you* think of, Alicia!" she said. "No wonder the Pi Sisters glare at you in Prayers each morning. I bet they'll watch out for you to do something you shouldn't, and tell on you."

"And I bet I'll get the better of them!" said Alicia, grimly. "If they try any tricks on me, I'll try a few on them!"

35

"Oh, do, do," begged Darrell, who had a great weakness for jokes and tricks. She didn't always dare to do them herself, but she was always ready to back up any one else who did.

Darrell soon got to know all the different classrooms too. She knew the art-room, with its clear north light. She hadn't yet had a lesson in the lab. or laboratory, which looked a bit frightening. She loved the great gym. with all its apparatus of swings, ropes, vaulting-horses and mattresses. She was good at gym. So was Alicia, who could climb like a monkey, and was as strong as a horse. Mary-Lou, of course, was too scared to do anything unless she was made to.

It was fun, the way all the girls slept in the Towers, and had their lessons in the other parts of the great building. Darrell knew where the teachers lived now in the building facing south, except those who, like Miss Potts, and Mam'zelle, lived in with the girls, to keep an eye on them. She began to wonder how she could have felt so lost and over-awed when she first arrived. She didn't feel a bit like a new girl now.

One of the things that Darrell liked best of all was the big swimming-pool down by the sea. This had been hollowed out of a stretch of rocks, so that it had a nice rocky, uneven bottom. Seaweed grew at the sides, and sometimes the rocky bed of the pool felt a little slimy. But the sea swept into the big natural pool each day, filled it, and made lovely waves all across it. It was a sheer delight to bathe there.

The coast itself was too dangerous for bathing. The tides were so strong, and no girl was allowed to swim in the open sea. But anyone was safe in the pool. One end was quite deep, and here there were diving-boards and a chute, and a fine spring-board for running dives.

Mary-Lou and Gwendoline were terrified of the pool, Mary-Lou because she was afraid of water, any-how, and Gwendoline because she hated the first cold plunge. Alicia's eyes always gleamed when she spied the shivering Gwendoline, and the poor girl so often had an unexpected push into the water that she soon began to step in hurriedly whenever she saw Alicia or Betty coming near.

The first week went very slowly. There was a lot to learn and know, things were so new and exciting. Darrell loved every minute, and soon got into the way of things. She was naturally quick and responsive, and the girls soon accepted her and liked her.

But they neither accepted nor liked poor Gwendoline, and as for Sally Hope, after trying in vain to draw her out a little, and get her to talk of her family and home, the girls let her live in her shell, and not come out of it at all.

"First week gone!" announced Alicia, some days later. "The first week always crawls. After that the days fly, and it's half-term in no time, and when that's gone we're looking forward to the hols. You've soon settled in, haven't you, Darrell?"

"Oh, *yes*," said Darrell. "I love it. If every term is as nice as this, I shall be thrilled!"

"Ah, you wait," said Alicia. "Everything's always all right at first – but when you've had a wigging or two from Mam'zelle, and been dosed by Matron, and kept in by Potty, and slated by Miss Remmington, and ticked off by one of the older girls, and . . . !"

"Oh, stop!" cried Darrell. "Nothing like that will happen, Alicia. Don't try and frighten me!"

But Alicia was right, of course. Things were not going to be quite as smooth and easy as Darrell thought!

Sally was sitting on the grass alone

Darrell had good brains and she had been taught how to use them. She soon found that she could easily do the work of her class, and in such things as composition was ahead of most of the others. She felt pleased.

"I thought I'd have to work much harder than at my old school," she thought to herself. "But I shan't! It's only maths. I'm not so good at. I wish I was as good as Irene at maths. She does things in her head that I can't even do on paper."

So, after the first week or two, Darrell relaxed a little, and did not worry herself too much about her work. She began to enjoy amusing the class a little, just as Alicia did. Alicia was thrilled to have someone to help her in her mischief.

Betty Hill went much further than Alicia. Darrell sometimes wondered if there was anything she would stop at. There were two mistresses that Betty and Alicia played up to. One was Mam'zelle Dupont, the other was a quiet, gentle mistress who took needlework, and sometimes took prep. time at night. Miss Davies never seemed to realize that Alicia and Betty could play tricks on her. Mam'zelle did realize it, but was taken in all the same.

"Did you ever hear how Betty put a white mouse into Mam'zelle's desk one day?" said Alicia. "Poor little thing, it couldn't get out, and suddenly, in despair, it pushed up the little ink-pot and stuck its nose out of the ink-pot hole. Mam'zelle nearly had a fit."

"What did she do?" asked Darrell, with great interest.

"Flew out of the room as if a hundred dogs were after her!" said Alicia. "When she was gone we took the mouse out quickly, and Betty hid it down her neck.

So when Mam'zelle ventured back, and ordered one of us to turn her desk out and get the mouse, there was none to be found. Mam'zelle thought her eyes had gone wrong!"

"Oh, I *do* wish I'd been there!" sighed Darrell. "Alicia, *do* do something funny like that. Do something in maths., can't you? I know Miss Potts is going to go for me over my maths. prep., and something like that would take her mind away from me!"

"What! Play a trick like that in Potty's class!" said Alicia, scornfully. "Don't be silly. Potty's up to everything. You can't fool *her*!"

"Well – in Mam'zelle's class, then," begged Darrell. "I like Mam'zelle, but I haven't seen her in a temper yet and I'd like to. *Do,* do play a trick in her class."

Alicia felt that she would have a most admiring spectator in Darrell, if only she could think of something. She screwed her forehead into wrinkles and thought hard.

Betty prompted her. "Can't you think of something Sam or Roger or Dick did last term?" she asked. She turned to Darrell. "Alicia's three brothers all go to the same school," she said. "And there's a master there called Toggles – at least that's what the boys call him – and he's such a dud the boys can play any trick they like on him and get away with it."

Darrell thought Roger, Sam, and Dick sounded fine brothers to have. She wished she had a brother too. But she had only a younger sister.

"There's one thing Roger did last term that was quite funny," said Alicia, suddenly. "I believe we could do it. But you and Betty will have to help, Darrell."

"Oh, I'd *love* to," said Darrell. "What is it?"

"Well, Roger pretended to be deaf," said Alicia. "And everything old Toggles asked him he pretended to hear wrong. When Toggles said 'John, sit still in your chair!' Roger said 'Give you a cheer sir? Certainly! Hip, hip, hip, hurrah!'"

Darrell laughed. "Oh, Alicia! That would be fun! Do, do pretend to be deaf, please do. We'll play up to you like anything. We will really. Do it in Mam'zelle's class."

The first form soon heard that Alicia was going to pull Mam'zelle's leg, and were thrilled. The first excitement of coming back to school had worn off. The girls were restless and ready for a bit of excitement.

"Now," said Alicia, "I'll pretend to misunderstand what Mam'zelle says – and then you can repeat it very loudly, Darrell, and then you, Betty, and then the rest of the class. See? We'll have some sport."

Mam'zelle, all unsuspicious of this deep-laid plot, entered the first-form classroom smiling brightly the next morning. It was a beautiful summer day. She had had two letters from home, giving her the news that she had a new little nephew. She had on a new brooch, and had washed her hair the night before. She was feeling in a very good temper.

She beamed round at the class. "Ah, my dear girls!" she said. "We are going to do some very very good French today, *n'est ce pas*? We are going to be better than the second form! Even Gwendoline will be able to say her verbs to me without one, single, mistake!"

Gwendoline looked doubtful. Since she had been at Malory Towers her opinion of her governess at home had gone down. Miss Winter didn't seem to have taught her half the things she ought to have known! On the other hand, thought Gwendoline, she had raved over her hair and blue eyes, she had praised the sweetness of Gwendoline's temper, and said how graceful she was in all she did. That kind of thing was most enjoyable to a person like Gwendoline. But a little more learning would have been very useful to her at Malory Towers.

She wished she had learnt a lot more French. Mam'-

zelle had exclaimed at the little she knew, and had even suggested extra French lessons in order to get her up to the average standard of the form. But so far Gwendoline had been able to avoid extra lessons, and she was quite determined to go *on* avoiding them! French five times a week was bad enough without extra time tagged on.

She smiled back rather doubtfully at Mam'zelle, hoping that Alicia would soon begin her performance, so that Mam'zelle's attention would not be directed at her. Mam'zelle beamed round again. She thought the girls looked eager and responsive this morning. The dear girls! She would tell them about her new little nephew. That would please them, no doubt!

Mam'zelle could never stop herself from talking about her beloved family in France, if she had had news of them. Usually the girls encouraged her, because the more they heard about *la chère* Josephine, and *la mignonne* Yvonne, and *la méchante* Louise, the less they heard about verbs and genders. So they were delighted when Mam'zelle informed them of her new nephew.

"*Il est appelé, Jean* – he is called John. *Il est tout petit, oh, tout petit*" Mam'zelle held up her two hands and measured a small distance between them to show how little her new nephew John was. "Now, what does that mean? *Il – est – tout – petit*. Who will tell me?"

Alicia was sitting in an atitude of strained attention, leaning forward as far as possible over her desk, one of her hands behind her ear. Mam'zelle noticed her.

"Ah, Alicia, you did not hear me very well? I will repeat. *Il – est – tout – petit*. Repeat to me, please."

"Pardon?" said Alicia, politely, and put both hands behind her ears.

Darrell wanted to giggle already. She tried to keep her face straight.

42

"Alicia! What is wrong with you?" cried Mam'zelle. "Can you not hear?"

"What do I fear? Why, nothing, Mam'zelle," said Alicia, looking slightly surprised. Somebody giggled and then smothered it quickly.

"Mam'zelle said 'Can you not *hear*?'" repeated Betty in a loud voice to Alicia.

"Beer?" said Alicia, more astonished, apparently, than ever.

"CAN YOU NOT HEAR?" shouted Darrell, joining in the game. And the class joined in too. "CAN YOU NOT HEAR?"

Mam'zelle banged on her desk. "Girls! You forget yourselves. What a noise to make in class."

"Mam'zelle, perhaps Alicia is DEAF," said Darrell, speaking as if Mam'zelle herself were deaf. "Maybe she has ear-ache."

"Ah, *la pauvre petite!*" cried Mam'zelle, who suffered from ear-ache herself at times, and was always very sympathetic towards anyone else who did. She bellowed at Alicia.

"Have you ear-ache?"

"A rake? I don't want a rake, thank you, Mam'zelle," replied Alicia. "I'm not gardening today."

This was too much for Irene, who let out one of her explosive laughs, making the girls in front of her jump.

"*Tiens!*" cried Mam'zelle, jumping too, "what was that? Ah, you Irene – why do you make that extraordinary noise? I will not have it."

"Can't help sneezing sometimes, Mam'zelle," stuttered Irene, burying her nose in her handkerchief as if she was about to sneeze again. Curious noises came from her as she tried to choke back her giggles.

"Alicia," said Mam'zelle, turning back to the mischiefmaker, who at once put both hands behind her ears, and frowned as if trying her best to hear. "Alicia, do not talk to me of rakes. Tell me, have you a cold?"

"No. I've no gold, only a ten-shilling note," answered Alicia, much to Mam'zelle's mystification.

"Mam'zelle said COLD not GOLD," explained Darrell at the top of her voice.

"You know – COLD, the opposite of HOT," went on Betty, helpfully. "Have you a COLD?"

"HAVE YOU A COLD?" roared the class, coming in like a well-trained chorus.

"Oh, *cold*! Why don't you speak clearly, then I should hear you," said Alicia. "Yes – I've had a cold, of course."

"Ah – then it has affected your poor ears," said Mam'zelle. "How long ago was this cold, Alicia?"

Darrell repeated this question at the top of her voice, followed by Betty.

"Oh – when did I have it? About two years ago," said Alicia. Irene buried her nose in her hanky again. Mam'zelle looked a little blank.

"It is of no use the poor child trying to follow the French lesson," said Mam'zelle. "Alicia, sit by the window in the sun and read your French book to yourself. You cannot hear a word we say."

Alicia looked enquiringly at Darrell, as if she hadn't heard. Darrell obligingly repeated it all at the top of her voice. Betty unfortunately was too overcome by a desire to laugh to be able to repeat it too. But the rest of the class obliged with a will.

"YOU CANNOT HEAR A WORD WE SAY!" they chorused.

The door opened suddenly and a most irate Miss Potts looked in. She had been taking Form 2 next door, and could not imagine what the shouting was in Form 1.

"Mam'zelle, excuse my interrupting you, but is it necessary for the girls to repeat their French lesson so very loudly?" she asked.

"Ah, Miss Potts, I am so sorry. But it is not for me

the girls repeat words so loudly, it is for the poor Alicia," explained Mam'zelle.

Miss Potts looked most surprised. She looked at Alicia. Alicia felt uncomfortable. She also looked as innocent as she could. But Miss Potts was always on the alert when Betty or Alicia looked innocent.

"What do you mean, Mam'zelle?" she snapped. "Has Alicia suddenly gone deaf? She was all right this morning."

"She is quite, quite deaf now," Mam'zelle assured her. Miss Potts looked sharply at Alicia.

"Come to me at Break, Alicia," she said. "I would like a few words with you."

Nobody dared repeat these words to Alicia, but Mam'zelle herself obliged. She shouted across to Alicia.

"Miss Potts says, will you . . ."

"Don't bother to repeat what I said, Mam'zelle," said Miss Potts. "Alicia will come all right. I shall expect you at eleven, Alicia. And please stand up when I speak to you."

Alicia stood up, her face a flaming red. Miss Potts went out of the room, and she did not shut the door very quietly. Mam'zelle disliked people who banged doors.

"Ah, this door, it goes through my poor head!" she said. "Miss Potts, she is very good and clever, but she does not have the head-ache, as I do . . ."

"Nor the ear-ache," put in Darrell, but no one raised a giggle. Miss Potts's entry and fierceness had damped the cheerfulness of the class considerably.

Alicia said no more about her ear-ache. She took a book and sat down by the window in the sunshine, feeling sure that Miss Potts would not appear again. She thought she might as well get something out of her performance! Mam'zelle took no further notice of her, and devoted herself to a whole-hearted search for someone in Form 1 who could and would conjugate

45

a whole French verb properly. Not finding anyone really good, she lost the good temper she had entered with that morning, and gave the class a bad time.

She stalked out when the bell for Break went. The girls crowded round Alicia. "Oh, Alicia! I nearly died when you said 'beer'." – "Wasn't it a shame Potty coming in like that?" – "Will you get into a fearful row, Alicia?"

"Darrell nearly yelled the roof off!" said Irene. "I almost burst with trying not to laugh."

"I must go and hear what Potty has to say," said Alicia. "Pity I forgot she was taking Form 2 next door! So long, girls!"

Darrell Loses Her Temper

Alicia got a good scolding, and extra prep. She came out from Miss Potts's room, and ran straight into Mam'zelle. "Have you been to see Miss Potts, Alicia?" asked Mam'zelle, thinking that perhaps Alicia hadn't heard what Miss Potts had said.

"Oh, yes, thank you, Mam'zelle," said Alicia, and walked off. Mam'zelle stared after her. How queer! Alicia had heard perfectly what she had said. Could ears get better so quickly then? Mam'zelle stood still and frowned. Miss Potts came out of her room and saw her.

"If Alicia shows any further signs of deafness, send her to me," said Miss Potts, coldly. "I can always cure it at once."

She walked off. Mam'zelle began to breathe quickly. "The bad girl, Alicia! – She has pulled my foot," said Mam'zelle, who sometimes got a little mixed! "She has hoodlewinked me! Never again will I believe her, the bad girl."

Darrell had thoroughly enjoyed the absurd affair. How cleverly Alicia had pulled it off! She looked at her admiringly, and Alicia liked the admiration. It always egged her on to further misbehaviour. Mary-Lou stared at her too, as if she was somebody most remarkable. Alicia went up and took Darrell's arm.

"We'll think of something else soon," she said. "You and I and Betty. We'll be the Bold Bad Three, or something like that!"

"Oh, *yes*!" said Darrell, thrilled at the idea of being one of a gang with Betty and Alicia. "Do let's! Maybe I could think of something, too."

It was decided, however, that it would be best not to try anything further until a little time had gone by. Perhaps something could be tried on Miss Linnie next.

Gwendoline was jealous of the way Alicia and Betty, recognized leaders in the first form, had made friends with Darrell. After all, Darrell was as new as she herself was. And she, Gwendoline, was much prettier, and had, she was sure, much more charm of manner.

She took Sally Hope into her confidence. "I don't like the way Darrell Rivers pushes herself forward all the time, do you?" she said to Sally. "Thinking she's so marvellous! Chumming up with Alicia and Betty. Not that I would if they asked me."

Sally didn't look very interested, but Gwendoline didn't mind. She went on grumbling about Darrell. "She thinks she's got such good brains, she thinks she plays such a marvellous game of tennis, she thinks she's so good at swimming! I've a good mind to show her that I'm *twice* as good as she is!"

"Well, why don't you?" said Sally, bored. "Instead of showing everyone you're twice as bad!"

Gwendoline was annoyed. To think that the quiet little Sally Hope should say such a thing to her! She looked at Sally as if she would like to wither her up.

"All right," said Gwendoline, grandly. "I *will* just

47

show you, Sally. I haven't really tried before, because it didn't seem worth it. *I* didn't want to come to Malory Towers, and Mother didn't want me to either. It was Daddy that made me come. I did marvellously with my governess, Miss Winter, and I could do marvellously now, if only I thought it was worth while!"

Alicia came up and heard this curious speech. She laughed loudly.

"You can't play tennis, you can't swim, you squeal when your toe touches the cold water, you don't even know all your twelve times table, baby! And then you talk of it not being worth while to show what you can do! You can't do a thing and never will, whilst you have such a wonderful opinion of yourself!"

Sally laughed too, and that made Gwendoline angry. How she would like to slap them both! But Miss Winter had always said that a little lady kept her hands to herself. Anyway, it would be decidedly dangerous to slap Alicia.

Gwendoline walked off, her nose in the air. "Dear Gwendoline Mary," remarked Alicia, in a loud voice. "Mummy's pet, Daddy's darling, Miss Winter's prize pupil. And can't do fractions properly yet!"

That evening the girls were in the swimming-pool, having a lovely time. Alicia swam under water the whole width of the pool, and then back again. Everyone applauded her.

"How *can* you hold your breath all that time?" cried Darrell. "I wish I could! Do it again, Alicia, when you've got your breath."

"The water's got properly into my ears this time!" said Alicia, shaking her head violently. "They feel all bunged up. I'll wait till they're clear. I'll do a spot of diving."

She was just as good a diver as a swimmer. Gwendoline, paddling about in the shallow end, envied her. She was certain *she* could swim and dive better than

Alicia – if only she could get over the unpleasant beginnings. She did hate the first cold plunge. She couldn't bear going under the water. She spluttered and gasped if she got water up her nose, and felt as if she was drowning.

There was only one person worse than she was, and that was poor Mary-Lou. No one teased Mary-Lou too much. It was too like teasing a small, bewildered kitten. Gwendoline saw her floundering about near her, and, because she knew Mary-Lou was even more afraid of the pool than she was, she felt a sense of power.

She waded over to Mary-Lou, jumped on her suddenly and got her under the water. Mary-Lou had no time to scream. She opened her mouth and the water poured in. She began to struggle desperately. Gwendoline, feeling the struggles, spitefully held her under longer than she had intended to. She only let her go when she felt a sharp slap on her bare shoulder.

She turned. It was Darrell, trembling with rage, looking as if she was shivering, so great was her anger. "You beast!" shouted Darrell. "*I* saw you duck poor Mary-Lou – and you know how scared she is. You nearly drowned her!"

She pulled Mary-Lou to the surface, and held her there, gasping and choking, blue in the face, almost sick with the amount of salt water she had swallowed.

Girls began to swim across to the scene of excitement. Darrell, her voice shaking with rage, addressed Gwendoline again. "You just wait a minute! I'll duck *you* under, Gwendoline, and see how *you* like it!"

Mary-Lou was clinging with all her might to Darrell. Gwendoline, rather scared by the anger in Darrell's voice, thought it would be just as well if she got out of the pool before Darrell or somebody else carried out the threat. She began to wade towards the steps that led down into the pool.

Just as she was climbing up them, Darrell, who had

given the weeping Mary-Lou to Alicia, caught her up.

"I'm not going to duck you, you little coward!" she cried. "But I *am* going to show you what happens to people like you!"

There came the sound of four stinging slaps and Gwendoline squealed with pain. Darrell's hand was strong and hard, and she had slapped with all her might, anywhere she could reach as Gwendoline hastily tried to drag herself out of the water. The slaps sounded like pistol-shots.

"Hey, Darrell!" came the voice of the head-girl of her dormy, Katherine. "Stop that! What are you thinking of? Leave Gwendoline alone!"

Still blazing, Darrell rounded on Katherine. "Somebody's got to teach that cowardly Gwendoline, haven't they?"

"Yes. But not *you*," said Katherine, coolly. "You put yourself in the wrong, slapping about like that. I'm ashamed of you!"

"And *I'm* ashamed of *you*!" burst out Darrell, much to everyone's amazement. "If *I* were head-girl of the first form I'd jolly well see that girls like Gwendoline learnt to swim and dive and everything, and left people like Mary-Lou alone. See?"

No one had ever seen Darrell in a temper before. They stared. "Get out of the pool," ordered Katherine. "Go on, get out. It's a good thing no mistress saw you doing that."

Darrell got out, still trembling. She went to where she had flung down her towel-cloak and put it round her. She climbed up the cliff slowly, her heart pounding.

Hateful Gwendoline! Horrid Katherine! Beastly Malory Towers!

But before she reached the top of the cliff and came to the little gate that led into the grounds of Malory Towers, Darrell's anger had all gone. She was dismayed. How *could* she have acted like that? And she had

50

absolutely *meant* always to keep her temper now, and never let that white-hot flame of rage flare up as it used to do when she was smaller.

Very much subdued, Darrell went back to the school, dried herself and changed. She had been publicly scolded by Katherine. Nobody had backed her up at all, not even Alicia. She had shouted at the head-girl of her form. She had behaved just as badly to Gwendoline as Gwendoline had behaved to Mary-Lou – except that it must have been sheer cruelty that made Gwendoline almost drown Mary-Lou, and it was anger, not cruelty, that made her slap Gwendoline so hard. Still – anger was cruel, so maybe she *was* just as bad as Gwendoline.

She felt sorry she had slapped Gwendoline now. That was the worst of having such a hot temper. You did things all in a hurry, without thinking, and then, when your temper had gone, you were terribly ashamed, and couldn't manage to feel better until you had gone to say you were sorry to the person you had hurt, and whom you still disliked heartily.

Darrell heard somebody sniffling in the changing-room. She looked to see who it was. It was Gwendoline, dolefully examining the brilliant red streaks down her thighs. That was where Darrell had slapped her. Gwendoline sniffed loudly.

"I shall write to tell Mother," she thought. "If only she could see those red streaks – why, you can see all Darrell's fingers in this one!"

Darrell came up behind her and made her jump. "Gwendoline! I'm sorry I did that. I really am. I was just so awfully angry I couldn't stop myself."

Gwendoline was neither generous nor gracious enough to accept such a natural apology. She drew herself up and looked at Darrell as if she smelt nasty.

"I should hope you are sorry!" she said contempt-

51

uously. "I shall write and tell my mother. If she thought girls at Malory Towers would behave like you do, she'd never have sent me here!"

Darrell – and Gwendoline

The girls left in the pool discussed the sudden happenings with interest and much surprise.

"Who would have *thought* quiet old Darrell would have lashed out like that!"

"She can't be allowed to cheek Katherine. That was jolly rude of her."

"Katherine, are you going to do anything about it?"

Katherine was now out of the pool, her usually calm face red and disturbed. She had liked Darrell so much – and now in one minute she had quite a different idea of her! Alicia was puzzled too. She shook her head from side to side, trying to get the water out of her ears. Who would have thought Darrell had such a temper?

"Come into the common room, North Tower girls, as soon as you are dressed," said Katherine at last, in her usual cool voice. The girls looked at one another. A first-form meeting! About Gwendoline and Darrell, they supposed. They tore off up the cliff, and poured into the changing-room, chattering loudly. Neither Gwendoline nor Darrell was there.

Gwendoline had gone up to her dormy, to get some cold cream for her red-streaked legs. They didn't need cold cream, of course – but she meant to make as much fuss as she could! She had always been jealous of Darrell, and she was jolly glad she had got something against her. Coming up and apologizing like that – she didn't mean a word of it, Gwendoline was sure!

The rest of the first-form North Tower girls, eight

of them, met in the common room. Katherine sat herself on a desk and looked round.

"I am sure you are all agreed that, much as we like Darrell, we can't pass behaviour of that sort," she began.

"Oh, Katherine – don't row her!" begged Mary-Lou's small voice. "She saved me from drowning, she really did."

"She didn't," said Katherine. "Gwendoline isn't such an idiot as to drown anyone. I suppose she just suddenly felt spiteful after being teased by the others for not trying to swim properly."

Mary-Lou was firmly convinced that Darrell was a heroine. She had suffered such agonies under the water, and had really and truly thought she was drowning – and then along had come strong, angry Darrell. How could Katherine judge her anyhow but kindly? Mary-Lou didn't dare to say any more, but she sat with a worried, anxious look on her face, wishing she could speak up for Darrell bravely and fearlessly. But she couldn't.

"I think," said Irene, "that Darrell should certainly apologize to Katherine for being cheeky to her. And if she won't, we'll send her to Coventry. We won't speak to her for a week. I must say I'm surprised at Darrell."

"Well, *I* think she must apologize to Gwendoline too," said Katherine. "I heard those slaps right at the other end of the pool! That's much more important than apologizing to me."

"But how *much* more unpleasant!" murmured Alicia. "How I should hate to have to say I was sorry for anything to darling Gwendoline Mary!"

"Aren't you going to address a few words to Gwendoline too?" asked Jean.

"Yes," said Katherine. "Of course. Now, I wonder where Darrell is. Oh, dear, I do hope she won't kick up a fuss about apologizing to Gwendoline. If she's still in a flaming temper she won't be easy to deal with. I don't *want* to report her, or to send her to Coventry. I never imagined she could be such a little spitfire."

Just as she finished this speech, the door opened and Darrell herself walked in. She looked surprised to see the girls sitting about, silent and serious. Katherine opened her mouth to speak to her, astonished to see Darrell looking so calm.

But before she could say a word, Darrell walked right up to her. "Katherine, I'm most awfully sorry I spoke to you like that. I can't think how I could. I was in such a temper, I suppose."

The wind was completely taken out of Katherine's sails. Instead of glaring at Darrell, she smiled. "That's all right," she said, rather awkwardly. "I saw you were in a rage. But, Darrell . . ."

"That's an awful fault of mine," said Darrell, rubbing her nose as she always did when she felt ashamed of herself. "My temper, I mean. I've always had it. I get it from Daddy, but he keeps his temper for something worth while – I mean he only loses it when there's some really big reason. I don't. I go and lose it for silly little things. I'm awful, Katherine! But honestly I had made up my mind when I came to Malory Towers that I wouldn't lose it any more."

The girls, who had looked coldly at Darrell when she had marched into the room, now regarded her with warm liking. Here was a person who had a fault, and who said so, and was sorry about it, and didn't attempt to excuse herself. Who could help warming to a person like that?

"Well," said Katherine, "you managed to lose it all right this evening! I think Gwendoline deserved all she got, Darrell – but you shouldn't have been the one to give it to her. I'm the one to tick her off, or Pamela, or even Miss Potts. Not you. Just imagine what the school would be like if we could all lose our tempers

54

and go about slapping people when we felt like it!"

"I know," said Darrell. "I've thought all that out myself. I'm much more ashamed of myself, Katherine, than you are of me. I wish you'd believe me."

"I do," said Katherine. "But I'm afraid, Darrell, you'll have to do something unpleasant, that you'll hate doing, before we can regard this matter as finished."

"Oh – what's that?" asked Darrell, looking really alarmed.

"Well, you'll have to apologize to Gwendoline," said Katherine, expecting an outburst from Darrell at once.

"Apologize to Gwendoline? Oh, I've done *that*," said Darrell, with relief. "I thought you meant I had to do something really awful. I'm always sorry very soon after I've lost my temper. I told you that. And that means I have to go and *say* I'm sorry!"

The girls stared at Darrell, who shook back her black curls and gazed with clear eyes at Katherine. Why, they hadn't needed to have a meeting at all! They hadn't needed to judge Darrell and set her to make amends. She had judged herself and made amends herself. The girls looked at her with admiration and Mary-Lou could hardly keep still. What a wonderful person Darrell was, she thought!

"Of course," went on Darrell, "I still think that Gwendoline did a beastly thing to Mary-Lou – and I think it's a pity too that Mary-Lou doesn't pull herself together so that spiteful people like Gwendoline can't tease her."

Mary-Lou crumpled up. Oh! Darrell thought her feeble and weak and frightened. And she was too. She knew she was. She knew that a strong person like Darrell could never really like a stupid person like Mary-Lou. But how she wished she would!

Gwendoline opened the door and came in, looking like a martyr. She had undone her hair so that it lay in a golden sheet over her shoulders again. She evidently fancied herself as an ill-used angel or something of the kind.

She heard the last few words that Darrell spoke, and flushed red. "Spiteful people like Gwendoline can't tease her!" That was what she heard.

"Oh – Gwendoline. The next time you want to give anyone a nasty fright, choose someone able to stand up to you," said Katherine, her voice sounding rather hard. "And please tell Mary-Lou you're sorry you were such a beast. You gave her an awful fright. Darrell has apologized to you, and you can jolly well do *your* bit, now!"

"Oh – so Darrell said she apologized to me, did she?" said Gwendoline. "Well, *I* don't call it an apology!"

"You fibber!" said Darrell, in amazement. She swung round to the girls. "I *did*!" she said. "You can believe which you like, me or Gwendoline. But I *did* apologize – straightaway too."

Katherine glanced from Darrell's hot face to Gwendoline's sneering one. "We believe *you*," she said, quietly. Her voice hardened again. "And now, Gwendoline, in front of us all, please, so that we can hear – what have you got to say to Mary-Lou?"

Gwendoline was forced to say she was sorry. She stammered and stuttered, so little did she want to say the words, but, with everyone's eyes on her, she had to. She had never said she was sorry for anything before in her life, and she didn't like it. She hated Darrell at that moment – yes, and she hated that silly Mary-Lou too!

She went out of the room almost in tears. There was a sigh of relief as she left. "Well, it's a good thing *that's* over!" said Irene, who hated scenes. "I'm off to one of the practice rooms. I feel a little music will be good after this upset!"

She went off to play the piano to herself in one of the many practice rooms. She would soon forget about everything but the melody she was playing. But the others didn't forget so easily. It hadn't been nice to see

Darrell lose control of herself, but everyone agreed that it served Gwendoline right to get a slapping.

The girls compared the natural, generous way in which Darrell had said she was sorry with the grudging, stammering words that Gwendoline had spoken to the embarrassed Mary-Lou. Gwendoline certainly hadn't come out of the affair at all well. And she knew it too. She felt humiliated. What a fuss to make over a joke! Why, the girls often ducked one another! Anyway, she *would* write to her mother about being slapped by that beast of a Darrell! That would make all the girls sit up.

She went back to the common room, and opened her locker. Her writing-paper was in there. She took out a pad and sat down. She did not usually enjoy writing to her mother. She thought it a bore! She had not written to Miss Winter at all since she had come to Malory Towers, though the governess had written to her three times a week. Gwendoline rather despised the people who liked her, and was spiteful towards those that didn't.

"I'm writing to my mother," she announced to the girls around. Some were sewing, some were reading. It was a free hour for them before supper-time. Nobody took any notice of Gwendoline's remark except Jean.

"Not the day for writing home, is it now?" she said. "What's come over you, Gwendoline, to be sending home in the middle of the week, when you sigh and groan over your Sunday letter fit to make us all hold our hands over our ears!"

"I'm writing to tell Mother how Darrell slapped me," said Gwendoline, clearly, so that everyone could hear. "I'm not going to stand that sort of thing. Mother won't, either."

Katherine got up. "I'm glad you told me what you were going to do," she said. "I'll go and get *my* writing-pad too. I am sure you won't tell your mother what led up to your slapping! But *I* will!"

Gwendoline flung down her pen in a fury. She tore the sheet she had begun, right off the pad and crumpled it up. "All right," she said. "I won't write. I'm not going to have you telling tales of me to my people. What a beastly school this is! No wonder Mother didn't want to send me away from home."

"Poor darling Gwendoline," said Alicia, as the angry girl flung out of the room. "She just can't do *any*thing she wants! I must say I think Malory Towers is going to be jolly good for her!" She shook her head violently again, and Darrell looked at her in surprise.

"Why do you keep doing that?" she asked.

"I told you. I can't seem to get the water out of my ears," said Alicia. "They feel blocked. I *say* – I do hope I shan't be deaf tomorrow! I did go deaf once before when I swam under water for ages!"

"Oh, Alicia! How funny it would be if you really did go deaf tomorrow in Mam'zelle's class!" said Darrell, heartlessly. "Oh, dear. I can't imagine what would happen!"

"Well, *I* can!" said Alicia. "Let's hope my ears get right before the morning!"

Alicia in Trouble

The affair at the Pool had a good many results. First, it made Mary-Lou follow Darrell about like a dog that has found its master and doesn't mean to leave it! She was always there to fetch and carry for Darrell. She tidied her desk for her. She even tidied the drawers in her dressing-table, and offered to make her bed each day.

But Darrell didn't like that sort of thing. "Don't," she said to Mary-Lou. "I can do things for myself. Why should you make my bed? You know we're all supposed to make our own, Mary-Lou. Don't be daft."

"I'm not," said Mary-Lou gazing at Darrell out of her big, wide eyes. "I'm only just trying to make a – a little return to you, Darrell – for – for saving me from drowning."

"Don't be silly," said Darrell. "You wouldn't have drowned, really. I know that now. And anyway I only slapped Gwendoline hard! That was nothing."

But it didn't in the least matter what Darrell said, Mary-Lou persisted in adoring her, and being on the watch for anything she could do. Darrell found chocolates put inside her desk. She found a little vase of flowers always on her dressing-table. But it irritated her and made her cross. She could not see Mary-Lou's timid reaching-out for a friendship that might help her. Mary-Lou was so weak. She needed someone strong, and to her Darrell was the finest girl she had ever met.

The others teased Darrell about Mary-Lou's attentions. "Has the little dog wagged its tail for you today?" asked Alicia.

"I wish *I* had some one to put bee-yoo-tiful flowers on my dressing-table!" said Irene.

"Just like Darrell to encourage silly nonsense like that!" said Gwendoline, who was jealous of all Mary-Lou's friendly little attentions to Darrell.

"She doesn't encourage it," said Katherine. "You can see she doesn't."

Another result of the Pool affair was that Gwendoline really did feel bitter towards Darrell now. She had never in her life been slapped by anyone, and she couldn't forget it. Not even her mother had slapped her! It would have been very much better for spoilt, selfish Gwendoline if a few smacks had come her way when she was small. But they hadn't, and now the four or five slaps she had received from Darrell seemed to her, not a sudden flash of temper, soon to be forgotten, but a great insult somehow to be avenged.

"And one day I'll pay her back, see if I don't!" thought Gwendoline to herself. "I don't care how long I wait."

The third result of the Pool affair was that Alicia really did go deaf through swimming under water so long. It was not a deafness that would last very long, Alicia knew. Suddenly her ears would go "pop" inside, and she would be able to hear as well as ever. But in the meantime it was really very annoying to think that just after she had *pretended* to be deaf, she really had become deaf. Whatever would Mam'zelle say this time?

It was unfortunate for Alicia that she sat at the back of the room, in the last row but one. Anyone with normal hearing could hear perfectly well, even in the back row, but Alicia with both ears "blocked," as she called it, found it extremely difficult to catch every word that was said.

To make matters worse, it was not Mam'zelle Dupont who took French that day, but Mam'zelle Rougier, thin, tall and bony. She was rarely in a good humour, as her thin lips, always tightly pressed together, showed. It was funny, Alicia thought, how bad-tempered people nearly always had thin lips.

Mam'zelle Rougier had a soft voice, which, however could become extremely loud when she was angry. Then it became raucous, like a rook's, and the girls hated it.

Today she was taking the beginnings of a French play with the girls. They nearly always had to learn one each term, taking different parts. Sometimes they performed it at school concerts, but often they didn't perform it at all, merely taking it in class.

"Now," said Mam'zelle Rougier, "today we will discuss the play, and perhaps give out the parts. Maybe one or two of the new girls are good at French, and can take the leading parts. That would be so nice!

I cannot think any of the old girls would mind that!"

They wouldn't! The less learning they had to do, the better! The new girls smiled in a sickly fashion. They thought Mam'zelle Rougier's little jokes were feeble.

"Now, first we will see who took the chief parts in last term's play," said Mam'zelle. "You, Alicia, what part did you play?"

Alicia didn't hear, so she didn't answer. Betty nudged her. "What part did you take in last term's play?" she said, loudly.

"Oh! Sorry, Mam'zelle, I didn't catch what you said," said Alicia. "I took the part of the shepherd."

"I thought that was in the term before," said Mam'zelle. Alicia again couldn't catch what she said. Betty repeated it loudly. "MAM'ZELLE SAID SHE THOUGHT THAT WAS IN THE TERM BEFORE," said Betty.

Mam'zelle was astonished. Why should Betty repeat everything she said like that? Then suddenly she remembered something Mam'zelle Dupont had told her about Alicia – ah, yes, the bad naughty girl! She had pretended to be deaf, hadn't she – and here she was again, playing the same trick on Mam'zelle Rougier.

"Ah non, non!" said Mam'zelle Rougier to herself angrily. "It is too much! I will not have it."

"Alicia," she said, patting the little bun at the back of her head, "you are a funny girl and you do funny things, n'est ce pas? But I also, I am funny and I do funny things. I would like you to write out for me in French, fifty times in your best handwriting, 'I must not be deaf in Mam'zelle Rougier's class.' "

"What did you say, Mam'zelle?" asked Alicia, having caught her own name at the beginning, but very little else. "I couldn't quite hear."

"Ah, cette méchante fille!" cried Mam'zelle, losing her temper as suddenly as she always did. "Alicia, écoutez bien! Listen well! You shall write me out 'I

61

must not be deaf in Mam'zelle Rougier's class' ONE HUNDRED TIMES!'"

"But you said fifty just now," said Betty, indignantly.

"And you too, you shall write out 'I must not interrupt,' one hundred times!" stormed Mam'zelle. The class was silent. They knew Mam'zelle Rougier in this mood. She would be handing out a thousand lines soon to somebody. She was the most irritable teacher in the whole school.

Betty whispered to Alicia as soon as Mam'zelle was writing something on the board, but, seeing that poor Alicia couldn't hear her whisper, she scribbled a message on a bit of paper.

"You've got to write out a hundred lines for M. For goodness' sake don't say you can't hear anything else, or you'll get a thousand! She's in a real paddy!"

Alicia nodded. And whenever Mam'zelle asked her if she had heard what was said, she answered politely, "Yes, thank you, Mam'zelle," hoping she would be forgiven for the story!

Miss Potts came for the next lesson. Mam'zelle stopped and spoke to her, with a gleam in her eye. "Alas, Miss Potts, one of your girls, Alicia, has again got a deafness in her ear. It is sad, is it not? Such a young and healthy girl!"

With this parting shot Mam'zelle Rougier disappeared. Miss Potts looked at Alicia coldly.

"I shouldn't have thought that even *you* were foolish enough to try the same trick twice, Alicia," she said. Poor Alicia! She didn't hear what Miss Potts said, but gazed at her inquiringly.

"You can leave your desk and come to one of the front ones," said Miss Potts. "Jean, change places with Alicia, please. You can change over the contents of your desk later."

Jean stood up, very pleased to think that she could leave the front row, which was always under Miss

Potts's eye, and go to one of the much-sought-after back rows. It was easy to whisper in the back row, and easy to play tricks or pass notes there. Alicia didn't move because she really hadn't heard. There was suddenly a curious buzzing noise in her ears.

"You've got to move, idiot!" said Betty in a loud whisper. "Go on – go to Jean's place."

Alicia realized what was happening. She was full of dismay! What, leave the back seat she liked so much, leave her seat beside Betty – and go to the front row, under every teacher's eagle eye. Everyone knew that the front row had no fun at all!

"Oh, Miss Potts," she began, in dismay. "Honestly, I *am* deaf! It's all that under-water swimming!"

"You thought – or pretended you were deaf the other day," said Miss Potts, unfeelingly. "How in the world am I supposed to know when you are and when you aren't, Alicia?"

"Well, I really *am* this time," said Alicia, wishing her ears wouldn't buzz so. "Please, Miss Potts, let me stay here!"

"Now, Alicia," said Miss Potts, speaking in loud, clear tones so that, deaf or not, Alicia would be sure to hear, "listen to me, and tell me if you agree with me or not. If you are *not* deaf, but playing a trick, it would be best to have you out here under my eye. If you *are* deaf and can't hear in the back row, then it is only common sense that you should be placed out here where you can. What do you think about it?"

Alicia, of course, could not do anything but agree. She sat rather sulkily down in Jean's place. She could, of course, hear much better there. Then a funny thing happened. First one of her ears went "pop" and then the other. She shook her head. Goody, goody! Her ears had gone pop and were all right again. She could hear as well as ever.

She was so pleased that she whispered to Mary-Lou,

next to her. "My ears have gone pop. I can hear!"

Miss Potts had extremely sharp hearing. She caught the whisper and turned round from the board. "Will you kindly repeat what you said, Alicia?" she said.

"I said 'My ears have gone pop. I can hear!'" said Alicia.

"Good," said Miss Potts. "I thought you would probably find you could hear all right in the front there."

"But Miss Potts, I . . ." began Alicia.

"That's enough," said Miss Potts. "Let us begin this lesson, please, without wasting any more time on your ears, deaf or not."

Alicia was cross because Jean and she had to change over the contents of their desks in Break. She hated being out in the front. Jean was very cheerful about the change.

"I wished hard enough I could be at the back," she said. "And now I am."

"It's not fair," grumbled Alicia. "I really *was* deaf this morning – and then my ears suddenly got right. Miss Potts ought to have believed me."

Darrell, who was helping, couldn't help laughing. Alicia was not in a mood to be teased, and she scowled.

"Oh, Alicia, I know it's unkind of me to laugh," said Darrell, "but honestly it's funny! First you pretend to be deaf, and pull Mam'zelle's leg well. Then you really *do* get deaf, and nobody believes it! It's just like that fable of the shepherd boy who called 'wolf wolf!' when there wasn't a wolf, and then, when there really was, and he called for help, nobody came because nobody believed him!"

"I thought you were my friend," said Alicia, stiffly. "I don't like being preached at."

"Oh, I'm not preaching, really I'm not!" said Darrell. "Listen, Alicia, I'll write out half your lines for you, I will really! It would take you ages to write out a hundred, and I know you hate writing. I love it."

64

"All right. Thanks very much," said Alicia, cheering up. So Mam'zelle Rougier was presented with one hundred lines that evening, half of them rather badly written and the other half quite nicely written. "Strange that a child should write so badly on one side of the paper and so well on the other!" said Mam'zelle wonderingly. But fortunately for Alicia Mam'zelle got no further than wondering about it!

A Queer Friendship

It was very hot. The girls simply lived for their time in the swimming-pool. They groaned when the tide was out and they couldn't bathe. Fortunately the pool was an enormous one, and would take practically the whole school when the tide was in.

Darrell loved to have a game of tennis and then sprint down to the pool to bathe. Oh, the delicious coolness of the water then! She couldn't understand how Gwendoline or Mary-Lou could possibly shrink from getting in. But they insisted that the hotter the day, the colder the water felt, and they didn't like it.

"But that's what's so *lovely* about the water," said Darrell. "Feeling so cold on such a blazing hot day as this! If you could only make up your minds to plunge in instead of going in inch by inch, you'd love it. You're awful cowards, both of you."

Neither Mary-Lou nor Gwendoline liked being called cowards. Mary-Lou always felt very hurt when Darrell so carelessly lined her up with Gwendoline, and scorned her, too, for her timidity. She tried her hardest to make Darrell pleased with her by running after her more than ever, even to tidying her locker in the common room, which exasperated Darrell because Mary-Lou always altered her arrangement of things.

"*What's* happened to my sweets? I *know* I put them in the front here. And where's my writing-pad? Blow, and I'm in such a hurry, too!"

And out would come every single thing in the locker, higgledy-piggledy on the floor! Mary-Lou would look on mournfully.

"Oh – I tidied them all so nicely for you," she would say.

"Well, *don't*!" Darrell would order. "Why don't you go and bother with somebody else's things? You always seem to make a bee-line for mine. You seem to have got a craze for tidying things and putting them away. You go and do Alicia's – they're much untidier than mine! Just leave mine alone!"

"I only do it to help you," Mary-Lou would murmur. It was awful to have such an admiration for somebody and for them to find it a nuisance. Perhaps Darrell *would* like her to tidy Alicia's things. She knew Darrell liked Alicia very much. Very well, then, she would help Alicia too.

But Alicia could not bear it any more than Darrell, and when poor Mary-Lou succeeded in breaking the glass of her mother's photograph, Alicia forbade her ever to touch any of her things again.

"Can't you *see* when you're a nuisance?" she said. "Can't you see we don't want a little ninny like you always flapping round us? Look at that photograph! Smashed to bits just because you started messing around."

Mary-Lou wept. She was always scared when anyone ticked her off. She went out of the room and bumped into Gwendoline in the passage.

"Hallo! Crying again! Whatever's up now?" asked Gwendoline, who was always interested in other people's rows, though never sympathetic.

"Nothing. It's only that Alicia and Darrell are always

66

so hard on me when I want to help them," wept poor Mary-Lou, feeling very sorry for herself.

"Oh, what do you expect from people like Alicia and Darrell – yes and Betty too?" asked Gwendoline, delighted to get in a few hard words about her enemies. "Always so cocksure of themselves, and so ready with their tongues. I can't imagine why you want to make friends with them."

"I've just broken a photograph of Alicia's mother," said Mary-Lou, wiping her eyes. "That's what the trouble was really about."

"Well, you may be sure Alicia won't forgive you for *that*," said Gwendoline. "She'll have her knife into you now. She just adores her mother, and nobody is ever allowed to handle that photograph. You've done it now, Mary-Lou!"

As she spoke, a perfectly wonderful idea came into Gwendoline's head. She stopped and thought a moment, her eyes shining. In one moment she saw how she could get even with Alicia and Darrell, yes, and give that stupid little Mary-Lou a few bad moments too. Mary-Lou looked at her curiously.

"What's the matter, Gwendoline?" she asked.

"Nothing. Just an idea," said Gwendoline. To Mary-Lou's intense surprise she suddenly slipped her arm through the younger girl's.

"You be friends with *me*," she said, in a honeyed voice. "*I* shan't treat you like Darrell does, and Alicia. I haven't a wicked tongue like Alicia, or scornful eyes like Darrell. Why don't you make friends with me? *I* shouldn't jeer at you for any little kindnesses, I can tell you."

Mary-Lou looked at Gwendoline doubtfully. She really didn't like her, but Gwendoline smiled at her so sweetly that she felt grateful. And Alicia and Darrell really *had* been horrid to her when she had tried to do things for them. Then she remembered how Gwendoline had held her under the water.

She took her arm away from Gwendoline's. "No," she said, "I can't be friends with you, Gwendoline. You were very cruel to me that day in the pool. I've had dreams about it ever since."

Gwendoline was angry to think that the stupid, feeble little Mary-Lou should refuse to be friends with her. But she still went on smiling sweetly. She took Mary-Lou's arm again.

"You know I didn't mean anything that time in the pool," she said. "It was just a joke. You've often seen the others being ducked. I'm sorry I ducked you so hard. I didn't realize you were so frightened."

There was something very determined about Gwendoline, when she had made up her mind about anything. Mary-Lou didn't know how to get away. So, as usual, she surrendered.

"Well," she said, hesitatingly, "well – if you *really* didn't mean to hurt me, that time in the pool, Gwendoline, I'll be friends. But I'm not going to talk against Darrell or Alicia."

Gwendoline gave her arm a squeeze, bestowed another honeyed smile on the perplexed Mary-Lou and walked off to think out her suddenly conceived plan in peace.

"It's marvellous!" she thought. "Everyone knows how fed-up Darrell is with Mary-Lou, because she's always tagging after her, and soon everyone will know how cross Alicia is because she has broken her mother's photograph. So, if *I* start playing a few tricks on Mary-Lou, everyone will think it is Darrell or Alicia getting back at her! And oh, goody, goody, Alicia has to sit by Mary-Lou now! That makes it easier still."

She sat down in the Court and thought out her plan. She meant to revenge herself on the three people she disliked. She would scare Mary-Lou to death – but she

68

would make everyone think it was Alicia and Darrell! Then they would be blamed, and punished.

"And if I make close friends with Mary-Lou nobody would ever *think* I had anything to do with things," thought Gwendoline, in delight. "Really, I'm very clever. I bet no one else in the whole of the first form could think of a plan like this."

She was right. They couldn't – but not because they weren't clever enough – but just because they weren't mean enough. Gwendoline couldn't see that. She couldn't even see that she was doing a mean thing. She called it "giving them all a lesson!"

She laid her plans very carefully. She would wait her time, till Alicia or Darrell were carrying out the duty of tidying the classroom and filling the vases with water. Then everyone would know they and they only had been in the classroom and so had the opportunity of slipping anything into anyone's desk, or taking something out.

She would pop a blackbeetle into Mary-Lou's desk – or a few worms – or even a mouse if she could get hold of it. But no – Gwendoline quickly ruled out mice because she was so scared of them herself. She didn't much like blackbeetles or worms either, but she could manage to scoop those up into a match-box or something.

She could do that. And she could remove Mary-Lou's favourite pencils and hide them in Alicia's locker. That would be a cunning thing to do! She might put one or two of Mary-Lou's books in Darrell's locker too. And how sympathetic she would be with Mary-Lou when she found out these tricks!

Gwendoline began poking round the garden to see what insects she could find. Jean, who was a good gardener, and liked to give a hand with the school garden at times, was most amazed to see Gwendoline poking about in the beds with a trowel.

69

"What *are* you doing?" she asked. "Looking for a bone you've buried?"

"Don't be silly," said Gwendoline, angry that Jean should have come across her. "Can't I do a little gardening? Are you to be the only one?"

"Well, what gardening are you doing?" demanded Jean, who always liked to know the ins and outs of everything that aroused her curiosity.

"Just digging," said Gwendoline. "Making the earth a bit loose. It's so dry."

Jean gave a snort. She had a wonderful variety of snorts, which she kept mainly for Gwendoline, Sally and Mary-Lou. Gwendoline dug viciously with her trowel, wishing she could put a worm down Jean's neck. But probably Jean wouldn't mind, anyway.

Gwendoline didn't like to look for worms after that. She decided to look for spiders. But when she saw a large one in the wood-shed she almost ran out helter-skelter herself! Still, it was *such* a large one, it would be just the thing for Mary-Lou's desk. It would come running out marvellously!

Somehow Gwendoline caught it, though she shivered as she clapped a flower-pot over it. She managed to get it into a little cardboard box. Then, feeling very clever, she slipped away to the common room, meaning to hide the spider in its box away in her locker until the right moment came.

She led the conversation round to spiders that evening. "I got my head caught in a web in the shed today," she said. "Oooh, it did feel horrid. I don't like spiders."

"My brother Sam once had a tame spider," began Alicia, who could always be relied on to produce a bit of family history at any moment. "It lived under a fern in our greenhouse, and it came out every evening for a drink of water, when Mother watered the ferns."

"Oooh! I should have hated to see it!" said Mary-Lou, with a shudder. "I'm terrified of spiders."

"You're an idiot," said Alicia, still cross over the broken photograph. "Terrified of this, scared of that — what a life you lead, Mary-Lou. I've a good mind to catch a large spider and put it down your neck!"

Mary-Lou turned pale. The very thought made her heart jump in fright. "I should die if you did that!" she said, in a low voice.

"Cowardy custard," said Alicia, lazily. "Well — wait till I get a spider!"

Gwendoline said nothing — but how she rejoiced! Could anything be better! Alicia had said more than she could possibly have hoped she would say — and what was more, every North Tower first-former had heard it. It was marvellous!

"I'll wait till Monday, when Alicia and Darrell are on duty in the classroom," she thought. "Then I'll do the trick. It will teach them all a lesson!"

So, when Monday came, Gwendoline watched for her moment. She and Mary-Lou went about everywhere together now, much to the surprise and amazement of Darrell and Alicia and Betty. How could Mary-Lou chum up with that awful Gwendoline, especially after that cruel ducking? And why was Gwendoline sucking up to Mary-Lou? It seemed very queer to the first-formers.

Gwendoline's chance came, and she took it. She was told to go and fetch something from her common room, ten minutes before afternoon school. She tore there to get it, then raced to the first-form classroom with the cardboard box. She opened it and let the great, long-legged spider run into the desk. It ran to a dark corner and crouched there, quite still.

Gwendoline hurried away, certain that no one had seen her. Two minutes later Darrell and Alicia strolled in to fill the flower-vases with water. Ah, luck was with Gwendoline just then!

The first lesson that afternoon was mental arithmetic. The girls groaned over this, except the quick ones, like Irene, who delighted in it. But it meant that there was no need for anyone to open a desk, because it was all oral work.

Miss Potts was lenient with the girls, for it was a very hot afternoon. Darrell was glad that Miss Potts was not as exacting as usual, for arithmetic was not her strong point, especially mental arithmetic.

The next lesson was to be taken by Mam'zelle Dupont. It was to be a French conversation lesson, in which the girls would endeavour to answer all Mam'zelle's simple questions in French. Miss Potts left, and Mam'zelle arrived, not quite so beaming as usual, because of the heat. She was too plump to enjoy the hot weather, and little beads of perspiration shone on her forehead as she sat down at the big desk, opposite the rows of girls.

"Asseyez-vous," she said, and the girls sat down thankfully, feeling that the only lesson they would really enjoy that weather would be a swimming lesson.

The lesson proceeded slowly and haltingly. The flow of French conversation was not at all brisk on the girls' part, and the constant pauses began to irritate Mam'zelle.

"Ah!" she cried at last, "it is too hot to make conversation with such stupid ones as you are this afternoon! Get out your grammar books and I will explain a few things to you that will help your conversation if you can get them into your so-stupid heads!"

The girls opened their desks to get out their grammar books. Gwendoline watched eagerly to see what would happen when Mary-Lou opened hers. But nothing did happen. Mary-Lou had neither seen the spider nor disturbed it. She shut her desk.

All the girls opened their grammar books at the page Mam'zelle commanded. Then Mary-Lou found that she had her English grammar instead of her French one. So she re-opened her desk to get the right book.

"*Que faites vous*, Mary-Lou?" demanded Mam'zelle, who hated desks being opened and shut too often. "What are you doing?"

Mary-Lou stuffed her English grammar into the back of her desk and pulled out the French one. The spider, feeling itself dislodged by the book, ran out in a fright. It ran almost up to Mary-Lou before she saw it. She let the desk-lid drop with a terrific bang and gave a heart-rending scream.

Everyone jumped in alarm. Mam'zelle leapt to her feet, sending a pile of books clattering from her desk to the floor. She glared at Mary-Lou.

"*Tiens!* What is this noise! Mary-Lou, have you gone mad?"

Mary-Lou couldn't speak. The sight of the enormous spider apparently running straight at her had completely undone her. She scraped her chair away from her desk, and stared at it as if she expected the spider to jump through the lid.

"Mary-Lou!" thundered Mam'zelle. "Tell me what is the matter with you? I demand it!"

"Oh, Mam'zelle – there's a – there's a simply enormous – giant – spider in my desk!" stammered Mary-Lou, quite pale.

"A spider?" said Mam'zelle. "And you make this fuss, and call out so loudly that we all jump in fear! Mary-Lou, be ashamed of yourself! I am angry with you. Sit down."

"Oh – I – I daren't," said Mary-Lou, trembling. "It might come out. Mam'zelle, it's enormous."

Mam'zelle wasn't quite sure whether she really believed in this spider or not. What with Alicia's deafness last week and one thing and another. . . .

Irene giggled. Mam'zelle fixed her with a glare. "We will see if this spider exists or not," she said, firmly. "And I warn you, Mary-Lou, if this is again a trick, and there is no spider, you will go to Miss Potts for punishment. I wash my hands of you."

She advanced to the desk. She threw open the lid dramatically. Mary-Lou drew in her breath and got away as far as she could, looking at the inside of the desk with scared eyes.

There was no spider to be seen. It had, of course, retreated to the darkest corner it could find again. Mam'zelle swept the desk with a searching glance and then turned on poor Mary-Lou.

"Bad girl," she said, and stamped her foot. "You, so quiet and good, you too deceive me, the poor Mam'zelle! I will not have it."

"Mam'zelle, *do* believe me," begged Mary-Lou, in despair, for she could not bear to be scolded like that. "It *was* there – an enormous one."

Mam'zelle rummaged violently among the books in the desk. "No spider! Not one!" she said. "Tell me, where has it gone, if it is still in there?"

The spider was alarmed by the violent rummaging. It suddenly hurried out from its hiding-place, and ran on to Mam'zelle's hand and up her arm.

Mam'zelle stared at the enormous thing as if she really could not believe her eyes. She gave a shriek even louder than Mary-Lou had given! She too was scared of spiders, and here was a giant specimen running over her person!

Irene exploded. That was the signal for the class to enter into the fun, and one and all scrambled over to Mam'zelle.

"Ah, where is it, the monster? Girls, girls, can you see it?" wailed Mam'zelle.

"It's here," said wicked Alicia and ran a light finger down Mam'zelle's spine. She gave a scream, thinking that it was the spider running there. "Take it off! I beg you, Alicia, remove it from me!"

"I think it must have gone down your neck, Mam'-zelle," said Betty, which nearly made Mam'zelle have a fit. She immediately felt sure that it was all over her, and began to shiver and tremble.

Alicia tickled the back of her neck and she leapt in the air. "Oh, la la! Oh, la la! What a miserable woman I am! Where is this monster? Girls, girls, tell me it is gone!"

There was now a complete uproar in the first-form room. Miss Potts, again in the second-form room, was amazed and exasperated. What *could* her form be doing now? Had Mam'zelle left them alone, and had they all gone mad?

"Go on with your maps for a minute," she said to the second form, who were glancing at one another in astonishment, as they heard the noise from the first-form room. She left the room and went rapidly to the door of the first form.

She opened it and the noise hit her like something solid. Worse than Break, she thought grimly. At first she could not see any mistress there at all, and thought that the girls were alone. Then she caught sight of Mam'zelle's head in the middle of a crowd of girls. What *was* happening!

"Girls!" she said, but her voice went unheard. "Girls!"

Irene suddenly saw her and started to nudge everyone. "Look out – here's Potty," she hissed.

The girls flowed back from Mam'zelle as if they were water! In a trice every one was by her desk. Mam'zelle stood alone, trembling, wondering what was

75

happening. Where had that monster of a spider gone?

"Mam'zelle, really!" said Miss Potts, almost forgetting the rule the staff had of never finding fault with one another before the girls. "I simply cannot think what happens to this class when you take it!"

Mam'zelle blinked at Miss Potts. "It was a spider," she explained, looking up and down herself. "Ah, Miss Potts, but a MONSTER of a spider. It ran up my arm and disappeared. Ah-h-h-h! I seem to feel it everywhere."

"A spider won't hurt you," said Miss Potts, coldly and unfeelingly. "Would you like to go and recover yourself, Mam'zelle, and let me deal with the first form?"

"Ah non!" said Mam'zelle, indignantly. "The class it is good – the girls, they came to help me to get this monster of a spider. So big it was, Miss Potts!"

Miss Potts looked so disbelieving that Mam'zelle exaggerated the size of the spider, and held out her hand to show Miss Potts that it was at least as big as a fair-sized frog.

The girls had enjoyed everything immensely. What a French lesson! Gwendoline had enjoyed it too, especially as she was the cause of it, though nobody knew that, of course. She sat demurely in her desk, watching the two mistresses closely.

And then suddenly she felt something running up her leg! She looked down. It was the spider! It had left Mam'zelle a long time ago, and had secreted itself under a desk, afraid of all the trampling feet around. Now, when peace seemed restored, the spider wanted to seek a better hiding-place. It ran over Gwendoline's shoe, up her stocking and above her knee. She gave a piercing scream. Everyone jumped again. Miss Potts turned fiercely.

"Gwendoline! Go out of the room! How dare you squeal like that! No, don't tell me you've seen the spider. I'm tired of the spider. I'm ashamed of you all!"

76

A spider was running up her leg!

Gwendoline shook herself violently, not daring to scream again, but filled with the utmost horror at the thought of the spider creeping over her.

"It *was* the spider!" she began. "It . . ."

"GWENDOLINE! What did I tell you! I will NOT hear another word of the wretched spider!" said Miss Potts, raising her voice angrily. "Go out of the room. The whole class can go to bed one hour earlier tonight as a punishment for this shameful behaviour, and you, Gwendoline, can go two hours earlier!"

Weeping, Gwendoline ran from the room. As soon as she got outside she examined herself carefully and tremblingly to see if the spider was still anywhere about her. To her enormous relief she suddenly saw it running down the passage.

She leant against the wall. How tiresome of that spider to come to her, when it might have gone to any-one else! Now she had got to have double punishment. Still, she would soon put it about that Alicia and Darrell had planted the spider in Mary-Lou's desk! How sick-ening of Miss Potts to pounce on her like that. *She* couldn't help it if the spider came to her.

But perhaps after all it was a good thing that Miss Potts had come into the room and heard it all. Perhaps Gwendoline might even drop a hint to Miss Potts about Alicia and Darrell putting the spider in the desk.

Miss Potts came out of the room at this moment. She eyed Gwendoline with dislike.

"Miss Potts, the spider ran away down there," said Gwendoline, pointing, anxious to get back into Miss Potts's good books.

Miss Potts took not the slightest notice but swept into the second-form classroom, and the door shut. Gwendoline felt very small. Now what was she to do? Stay out here – or go back into the classroom? She didn't want to be found out there if by any chance Miss Grayling, the Head, came by. She decided to risk going back. She opened the door and sidled in.

"Ha! You are back again! And who told you to come?" demanded Mam'zelle, now ashamed of her part in the affair, and ready to vent her humiliated feelings on anyone she could. "You screamed and made Miss Potts white and angry!"

"Well, Mam'zelle, you screamed too," protested Gwendoline, in an injured tone. "Louder than I did, I should think."

Mam'zelle rose in her seat, and for all her smallness she seemed enormous to Gwendoline just then. Her beady black eyes flashed.

"You would be rude to *me*, Mam'zelle Dupont! You would argue with *me*, who have taught here for twenty years! You – you . . ."

Gwendoline turned and fled. She would rather stand outside the door all day long than face Mam'zelle when she looked like that!

Sharp Words

The Spider Affair, as it was called, went all over the school before the day was out. It caused a great deal of laughter. When Mam'zelle Rougier heard of it she sneered.

"To think that a Frenchwoman should be so foolish!" she said. "Now *I* do not mind spiders or ear-wigs or moths or even snakes! Mam'zelle Dupont should be ashamed to make such an exhibition of herself!"

The first form talked about it more than anyone else, of course. They squealed with laughter whenever they thought of poor Mary-Lou, Mam'zelle and Gwendoline all falling victims to the same spider.

"Jolly clever spider!" said Irene. "It knew the only

three people in the form that would be scared of it. I take my hat off to that spider."

"I can't think why it chose *my* desk," said Mary-Lou.

"No. That was a shame," said Gwendoline. "Poor Mary-Lou! It must have been an awful shock for you when you saw it. I wonder who put it there?"

There was a silence. For the first time it occurred to the first form that the spider might have been put there on purpose. They looked at one another.

"It was a dirty trick to put it into poor Mary-Lou's desk," said Jean. "She can't *help* being scared of things, I suppose, and she almost jumped out of her skin when she saw it. I should have thought any joker in our form would have been decent enough to have popped it into, say, Alicia's desk!"

"Not if it happened to be *Alicia* who popped it in!" said a sly voice. "You do so love playing tricks, don't you, Alicia? You and Darrell were in the first-form room before afternoon school. And I'm sure we all remember you saying you'd like to put a spider down Mary-Lou's neck!"

It was Gwendoline speaking. Alicia glanced at her. "Well, I didn't do it," she said. "Nor did Darrell. Sorry to disappoint you, darling Gwendoline Mary, but we just didn't. If it was anyone, I should think it was you!"

"Mary-Lou is my friend," said Gwendoline. "I wouldn't do that to her."

"Well, if you'd almost drown her one week, I should think you could quite well bring yourself to put a spider in her desk the next week," said Darrell.

"It's pretty funny that you and Alicia were the only ones in the classroom before afternoon school," persisted Gwendoline, angry that no one seemed to have agreed with her suggestion.

"Shut up," said Katherine, shortly. "We *know* it wasn't either Darrell or Alicia, because they *say* so!

The spider must have got in there by accident, and that's that."

"Well, *I* think . . ." began Gwendoline, but the class took up a chant at once.

"Shut up, Gwendoline; Gwendoline, shut up! Shut *up*, Gwendoline; Gwendoline, shut *up*!"

There was nothing to do but shut up. Gwendoline was sulky and exasperated. It had been such a good idea, and all that had resulted from it was a double punishment for her, and a complete failure to make anyone believe that Alicia or Darrell had played the trick. True, the first formers had had to go to bed an hour earlier, but they had all voted it was worth it.

Gwendoline felt vicious about the whole affair. She determined not to be put off by her first failure but to go on doing things to Mary-Lou, so that in the end the class would have to put them down to tricks by Alicia and Darrell. She thought too she would also hint to Miss Potts that she thought Alicia and Darrell were at the bottom of things.

But she didn't get very far with this. She had to go and see Miss Potts about some returned homework, and stood very meekly beside her, in the little room that Miss Potts shared with Mam'zelle Dupont at North Tower.

"Miss Potts, I was awfully sorry about that spider affair the other day," she began. "Of course, Alicia and Darrell were in the classroom beforehand, and I'm sure they know something about it. I heard Alicia say . . ."

Miss Potts looked up. "Are you trying to sneak?" she said. "Or in more polite language, to tell tales? Because if so, don't try it on me. At the boarding school I went to, Gwendoline, we had a very good punishment for sneaks. All the girls in the sneak's dormy gave her one good spank with the back of a hair-brush. You may have a lot of interesting things to tell me but it's no use expecting me to listen. I wonder if

81

the girls here have the same punishment for sneaks. I must ask them."

Gwendoline went flaming red. A sneak! Fancy Miss Potts daring to call her, Gwendoline Mary Lacey, a sneak! All because she had just wanted to drop a kindly hint. Gwendoline didn't know what to say. She felt as if she would like to burst into tears, but Miss Potts always got very impatient with girls who did that. She went out of the room, longing to slam the door as she often did at home. But she didn't dare to here.

She felt very sorry for herself. If her mother knew what an awful school she had come to she would take her away at once. Miss Winter, too, would be horrified. But Gwendoline wasn't quite so sure about her father. He could say things at times very like the things Miss Potts said.

The week went by. It was a very pleasant week, hot with a cool breeze that made games and swimming even more pleasure than usual. Alicia and Betty were practising hard for the school sports. Both were excellent swimmers and divers. Darrell tried to imitate all they did. She was good, too, but not quite so good as they were. But she was quite fearless, and dived off the highest diving-boards, and went down the chute in all kinds of peculiar positions.

The only unhappy person that week was Mary-Lou. She got into a lot of trouble over many little things. For instance, her clothes in the changing-room had been thrown down in a pool of water, and were soaking wet. She had to take them to Matron to be dried.

Matron was cross. "Mary-Lou! Can't you hang your things up properly in that changing-room? You know there are always puddles on the floor from the girls coming in and out from the pool."

"I did hang them up, Matron," said Mary-Lou, mildly. "I know I did."

Then Mary-Lou's tennis racket suddenly showed

three broken strings. They were not frayed, but looked as if they had been cut. Mary-Lou was upset.

"My new racket!" she said. "Look, Gwendoline, who would think a new racket could go like that?"

"It couldn't," said Gwendoline, pretending to examine it very closely. "These strings have been cut, Mary-Lou. Someone's been playing a dirty trick on you. What a shame."

Mary-Lou was miserable. She couldn't believe that she had any enemies. But when she found buttons cut off her Sunday dress she knew that someone was being unkind and mean. Gwendoline comforted her.

"Never mind. *I'll* sew them on for you! I hate sewing, but I'll do it for you, Mary-Lou."

So, making a great show of it, Gwendoline sewed on the six blue buttons one night. The first-formers stared at her in surprise. They knew she never mended anything if she could help it.

"How did those buttons come off?" asked Jean.

"That's what *I'd* like to know," said Gwendoline smugly. "Six buttons, all ripped off! I'm putting them on for Mary-Lou, because I'm so sorry that anyone should play her such a dirty trick. And I'd like to know who cut the strings of her tennis racket, too."

The first-formers looked at one another. It certainly was queer the way things had been happening to poor Mary-Lou lately. Even her prayer-book had disappeared. And some of her pencils had gone. True, they had been found in Alicia's desk – but everyone had thought that was just an accident. Now they began to wonder if some one had put them there. Not Alicia. Alicia wouldn't do a thing like that. But Somebody.

It was getting near half-term. Many of the girls were excited, because some of them were expecting visits from their parents. Any parent who lived not too far away would be sure to come. Darrell was thrilled because her father and mother were coming. They lived a long way away, but had decided to take a week's holiday in Cornwall, and come and see Darrell in the middle of it.

The girls began to talk about their families. "I wish my three brothers could come," said Alicia. "We'd have some sport then."

"I wish my little sister could come," said Jean. "I'd love to show her Malory Towers."

"Is *your* mother coming, Sally?" asked Mary-Lou.

"No," said Sally. "She lives too far away."

Darrell remembered something her mother had told her in a letter a week or two before. She had said that she had met Sally Hope's mother, and had liked her. She had said too that she had seen Mrs. Hope's baby, Sally's sister, a little girl of three months. Darrell had meant to tell Sally what her mother had said and had forgotten. Now she remembered it.

"Oh, Sally, I expect your mother won't come because of the baby," she said.

Sally went stiff. She stared at Darrell as if she couldn't believe her ears. Her face went quite white, and when she spoke she sounded as if she were choking.

"You don't know what you're talking about," she said. "What baby? We haven't a baby! My mother won't be coming because it's so *far,* I tell you!"

Darrell was puzzled. "But, Sally – don't be silly – my mother said in a letter that she had *seen* your baby sister – she's three months old, she said."

"I haven't *got* a baby sister!" said Sally, in a low, queer voice. "I'm the only one. Mother and I have been everything to each other, because Daddy has had to be away such a lot. I haven't *got* a baby sister!"

The girls looked at Sally curiously. Whatever could be the matter with her? She sounded so queer.

"All right," said Darrell, uneasily. "*You* ought to know, I suppose. Anyway, I expect you'd like a sister. It's nice having one."

"I should hate a sister," said Sally. "I wouldn't share my mother with anyone!"

She walked out of the room, her face as wooden as ever. The girls were really puzzled. "She's a funny one," said Irene. "Hardly ever says anything – all closed up, somehow. But sometimes those closed-up people burst open suddenly – and then, look out!"

"Well, I shall certainly write and tell Mother she's mistaken," said Darrell, and she did so, then and there. She told Sally the next time she saw her.

"I'm sorry I made that mistake about you having a sister," she said to Sally. "I've written to tell Mother you said you hadn't one. She must have mistaken what your mother said."

Sally stood still and glared at Darrell as if she suddenly hated her. "What do you want to go interfering for?" she burst out. "Leave me and my family alone! Little busybody, always sticking your nose into other people's affairs!"

Darrell's temper flared up. "I don't," she said. "You guard your tongue, Sally. I never meant to interfere, and I can't think what all the fuss is about. Either you have a sister or you haven't. *I* don't care."

"You tell your mother not to interfere either!" said Sally. "Writing letters about my family!"

"Oh, don't be so *silly*!" flared back Darrell, really exasperated now. "Anyone would think there was a deep, dark mystery, the way you go on! Anyway, I'll just see what my mother says when she next writes to me – and I'll tell you."

"I don't want to know. I won't know!" said Sally, and she put out her hands as if she was fending Darrell off. "I hate you, Darrell Rivers – you with your mother who comes to see you off, and sends you things and writes you long letters and comes to see you! And you boast about that to me; you do it all on purpose. You're mean, mean, mean!"

Darrell was utterly taken aback. What in the wide world did Sally mean? She watched the girl go out of the room, and sank down on to a form, completely bewildered.

Half-term at Last

The girls became very excited at the beginning of half-term week. Many of them would see their parents on the Saturday – and Miss Remmington, the games-mistress, had suddenly decided to have a small edition of the Swimming Sports for the benefit of the parents. Everyone who visited Malory Towers was struck with the beautiful natural pool, and loved to see it.

"So it would be nice this half-term, as it's so hot, for your people to go down to the breezy pool, and see not only the beauties of the water, but the way their girls can swim and dive!" said Miss Remmington. "We will have a pleasant time down there and then come back for a strawberry and cream tea, with ices!"

What fun! Darrell hugged herself with joy whenever she thought of it. She had got on so well with her swimming and diving, and she knew her parents would be pleased. And strawberries and ice-cream afterwards. How simply wizard!

But she was rather taken aback on Wednesday when the half-term places were read out. Instead of being in the first three or four, as she had hoped, she was tenth from the bottom. She could hardly believe her ears! Katherine was top, Alicia was fifth, Betty was four-teenth, Gwendoline was bottom – Mary-Lou was sixth from the bottom, not very far below Darrell!

Darrell sat very quiet whilst the rest of the marks were read out. There were thirty or so girls in her form – and more than twenty of them had done better than she had. Surely, surely there must be some mistake?

She went to Miss Potts about it, looking worried. "Miss Potts," she began, rather timidly, for the mistress was correcting papers and looked very busy, "Miss Potts, excuse my interrupting you, but can I ask you something?"

"What is it?" said Miss Potts, running her blue pencil across a line of writing.

"Well – it's about the form order," said Darrell. "Am I really so low down as that?"

"Let me see – what were you? Quite a long way down," said Miss Potts, pulling the list to her and looking at it. "Yes, that's right. I was surprised and disappointed, Darrell. You did so well in the first two weeks."

"But Miss Potts," said Darrell, and then stopped. She didn't know quite how to say what she wanted to say. She wanted to say that she had much better brains than at least half the form, so why was she so low? But somehow that sounded conceited.

However Miss Potts, who was very quick-minded, saw her difficulty. "You have come to ask me how it is you are nearer the bottom than the top when you could so easily be among the top ones?" she said. "Well, I'll tell you, Darrell. There are people like Alicia, who can play the fool in class and waste their time and everyone else's, and yet still come out well in their work. And there are people like you, who can also play the fool and waste their time – but unfortunately it affects their work and they slide down to the bottom. Do you understand?"

Darrell flushed very red and looked as if she could sink through the floor. She nodded.

"Yes, thank you," she said, in a small voice. She looked at Miss Potts out of her clear brown eyes. "I wouldn't have been so silly if I'd known it was going to affect my place in the form," she said. "I – I just thought

87

as I had good brains and a good memory I'd be all right, anyhow. Daddy and Mother will be disappointed."

"They probably will," said Miss Potts, taking up her pencil again. "I shouldn't copy Alicia and Betty too much if I were you, Darrell. You will be a finer character if you go along on your own, than if you copy other people. You see, what *you* do, you do whole-heartedly – so if you play the fool, naturally other things will suffer. Alicia is able to do two or three things quite well at one and the same time. That certainly has its points – but the best people in this world are the whole-hearted ones, if they can only make for the right things."

"I see," said Darrell. "Like my father. He's whole-hearted. He's a surgeon and he just goes in for giving back people their health and happiness with all his heart – so he's marvellous."

"Exactly," said Miss Potts. "But if he split himself up, so to speak, and dabbled in half a dozen things, he would probably not be nearly such a remarkable surgeon. And when you choose something worth while like doctoring – or teaching – or writing or painting, it is best to be whole-hearted about it. It doesn't so much matter for a second-rate or third-rate person. But if you happen to have the makings of a first-rate person and you mean to choose a first-rate job when you grow up, then you must learn to be whole-hearted when you are young."

Darrell didn't like to ask Miss Potts if she thought she had the makings of a first-rate person in her, but she couldn't help hoping that she had. She went away rather subdued. What a pity she hadn't been whole-hearted over her work and got up to the top, instead of being whole-hearted over playing the fool with Alicia and Betty, and sliding down towards the bottom.

Gwendoline's mother and her old governess, Miss Winter, were coming on Saturday too. Gwendoline was very much looking forward to showing off in front of them. How small she would make Miss Winter feel, when she talked of her lessons and how wonderful she was at everything!

Mary-Lou's people were not coming and she was disappointed. Gwendoline spoke kindly to her. "Never mind, Mary-Lou. You can keep with me and my mother and Miss Winter all day. I won't let you feel lonely."

Mary-Lou didn't much want to keep with Gwendoline. She was tired of being pawed about by Gwendoline, and tired of the never-ending stories of her family, in all of which Gwendoline herself shone out brightly as someone really too marvellous for words.

But Gwendoline thoroughly enjoyed such a quiet listener as Mary-Lou, though she despised her for being weak enough to put up with so much.

When Darrell heard that Mary-Lou's people could not come on half-term Saturday she went to her. "Would you like to come and be with my mother and father and me all day?" she said. "They are taking me out to lunch in the car. We're having a gorgeous picnic."

Mary-Lou's heart leapt. She gazed at Darrell in adoration and delight. To be asked by *Darrell* to share the half-term – could anything be nicer? Darrell had ticked her off so much lately, and found her such a nuisance – but now she had been decent enough to give her this invitation.

Then she remembered Gwendoline's invitation, and her face fell. "Oh," she said, "Gwendoline's asked me to join *her* – and I said I would."

"Well, go and tell her *I've* asked you, and that my father and mother would like to meet you," said Darrell. "I shouldn't think she'd mind."

"Well – I don't know if I dare say that," said timid Mary-Lou. "She might be very angry – especially as she doesn't like you, Darrell."

"I suppose that means you'd rather go with Gwendoline than with me," said Darrell, unkindly. It always irritated her when Mary-Lou put on her "scared" look. "Well, go then."

"*Darrell!* How can you say that?" cried Mary-Lou, almost in tears. "Why – I'd – I'd – I'd give *anything* to come with you."

"Well, go and tell Gwendoline then," said Darrell. "If you want a thing badly you can surely pluck up enough courage to get it. You're a terrible little coward."

"Oh, I know," said Mary-Lou, in despair. "Don't keep on and on saying that! It only makes me worse! *You* tell Gwendoline, Darrell."

"Certainly not," said Darrell. "*I'm* not going to do your dirty work! Anyway, I'm not sure I want such a silly baby tagging on to me all half-term."

She walked off, leaving Mary-Lou looking after her in despair. Jean, who was nearby and had overheard everything, felt a little sorry for Mary-Lou. She walked after Darrell.

"I think you're a bit hard on her," she remarked, in her forthright Scots voice.

"Well, it's all for her good," said Darrell. "If I can *make* her have a little courage, she'll thank me for it. I said those things purposely, to shame her into going to Gwendoline and asking her."

"You've shamed her all right, but not in the way that will make her pluck up her courage," said Jean. "You've given her the kind of shame that puts people into despair!"

Jean was right. Mary-Lou was quite in despair. The more she thought of going to Gwendoline and asking her if she minded her going with Darrell at half-term instead of with her, the more terrified she got. In the end she did go to find Gwendoline, but found that she didn't dare to ask her; which made it worse than ever! Poor Mary-Lou!

Gwendoline got to hear that Darrell had asked Mary-Lou for half-term, and she was pleased that Mary-Lou had not apparently wanted to go with her. She spoke to her about it.

"Fancy Darrell having the cheek to ask you, after *I'd* asked you!" she said. "I'm glad you had the decency to refuse, Mary-Lou. You'd surely not want to go off with a girl like that, who thinks you're such a poor worm?"

"No," said Mary-Lou, and couldn't say any more. If only she could have said yes, boldly, right out! But she couldn't.

The morning of half-term dawned bright and clear. It was going to be a super day. The sea glinted in the sunlight, as calm as a mirror. It would be high tide at two o'clock. The pool would be just right. What luck!

Girls took loads of camp-stools down to the pool and set them on the high rocky place above the pool, where the tide seldom reached. It was a fine place for watching. Darrell sang loudly as she went up and down, her heart leaping because she would see her parents that day. Mary-Lou did not sing. She looked sober and down-hearted. Sally Hope looked sober too – her face more "closed-up" than ever, thought Darrell.

Alicia was in high spirits. Her mother and father were coming and one of her brothers. Betty's parents were not coming, so she was, of course, going to be with Alicia.

Darrell, catching sight of Sally trudging up the cliff, after taking down some camp-stools, was struck by the sad expression on her face. Impulsively she hailed her.

"Hie, Sally! Sally Hope! Your people aren't coming, are they? Wouldn't you like to join me and my parents today? I can ask anyone I like."

"I'd rather not, thank you," said Sally, in a stiff little voice, and went on up the cliff without another word.

"Well, she *is* a funny girl," thought Darrell, feeling rather annoyed that the two girls she had so far asked hadn't either of them agreed to come with her. She went off to find someone else whose people were not coming. She really must get *some*body, because her mother had said she would like to take another girl out too. "Your own particular friend, if possible," her mother had written.

But Darrell hadn't got a "particular friend." She would so much have liked Alicia, but Alicia was Betty's friend. She liked Irene, too, but Irene never seemed to feel the need of a friend. Her music made up to her for everything.

"Oh, well – what about asking Emily?" thought Darrell. She was not at all interested in the quiet, studious Emily, who always seemed to be sewing most industriously every evening. But Emily's people weren't coming, and no one had asked her to go out to lunch with them.

So she asked Emily, who blushed with pleasure and said yes, she would be delighted to come. She seemed surprised that Darrell had asked her. Mary-Lou was almost in tears when she saw the two of them going off to get ready to meet Darrell's parents. She couldn't bear to think that Emily was going to have the treat she would so much have loved herself – but hadn't enough courage to get.

A Really Lovely Day

Soon the big drive in front of Malory Towers was crowded with cars of all shapes and sizes. Parents climbed out of them and looked for their girls. There were shrieks of delighted welcome all over the place.

"Mummy! Daddy! I'm so glad you've come early!"

"Mother! I didn't expect you so soon! Oh, it's lovely to see you again!"

Darrell was watching for her father and mother, too.

She soon saw her father's plain black car, which he drove himself. And there was mother sitting beside him, looking pretty in a new dress, and excited because she would so soon see Darrell.

Darrell shot out of the doorway and down the drive like an arrow, nearly knocking over Gwendoline, who was waiting impatiently for her own mother. She flung herself on her parents. "Mother! I've been waiting and waiting! Oh, it's lovely to see you again! Hallo, Daddy – did you drive all the way down?"

"Hallo, darling," said her mother and looked at her in pleasure. Darrell was brown and glowing with colour. Her warm brown eyes were filled with delighted love. She looked happy and "on top of the world" as her father put it to himself. Both her parents were pleased.

Darrell took them into the school, chattering at the top of her voice. "You must see my dormy. You must see the very bed I sleep in – and I *must* show you the view out of our dormy window. It's super!"

In her intense excitement she had forgotten all about Emily, waiting patiently nearby. She suddenly saw her, and stopped.

"Oh – Emily! Mother, you said I could choose some one to come out with us – and here she is. This is Emily Lake, a girl in my form."

Mrs. Rivers looked at Emily and was surprised. She had not expected a quiet sober little girl like this to be Darrell's chosen friend. She did not know that as yet Darrell had no definite friend. She shook hands with Emily, and said she was pleased she was coming out with them.

After that Emily tagged along behind them, listening to Darrell's excited chatter, and her parents' amused replies. She liked Darrell's parents. Her mother was pretty and amusing, and sensible too – and as for her father, well, any one would trust him at sight, thought Emily, gazing at his determined, good-looking face with

93

its big dark eyes and intensely black eyebrows, just like Darrell's but bigger and shaggier.

Darrell was proud of her parents. She wanted to show them off. She saw Gwendoline with two women – one obviously her mother, with bright golden hair like Gwendoline's and a rather babyish, empty face. The other must be Miss Winter, the governess, thought Darrell. What an awful person!

Poor Miss Winter was not really awful. She was plain and poor and always eager to agree with everyone. She adored Gwendoline because she was pretty and graceful, and did not seem to see the selfishness and spoilt ways of the silly little girl.

Mary-Lou was with them, trying to smile, but really very unhappy. She didn't like either Mrs. Lacey or Miss Winter and she was beginning to feel horrified at some of the fibs that she had heard Gwendoline tell them.

"I'm almost the best at tennis in our form," she heard Gwendoline say. "I shouldn't be surprised if I'm put into a match-team, Mother!"

"Oh, darling – how clever you are!" said Mrs. Lacey, fondly. Mary-Lou stared at Gwendoline in surprise. Why, everyone knew Gwendoline was a real muff at all games!

"And Mam'zelle is very pleased with my French," went on Gwendoline. "I believe I might be top in that. She says I have a splendid accent."

Miss Winter glowed. "Oh, Gwen darling! Isn't that lovely now? I did my best with you, of course, but I was always afraid it was rather a *poor* best, because I've never been to France."

Mary-Lou longed to say that Gwendoline was always bottom in the French class, but she did not dare to. How *could* Gwendoline stuff her people up with such a lot of lies? And how *could* they believe them?

"Are you going to go in for the swimming-match this afternoon?" asked Mrs. Lacey, looking fondly at

Gwendoline, who today had her shining golden hair loose down her back, and looked, so her mother thought, like a real angel.

"No, I thought I wouldn't, Mother," said Gwendoline. "It's best to give the others a chance. After all, I've done well at so many things."

"There's my sweet, unselfish girl!" said Mrs. Lacey, and squeezed Gwendoline's arm. Mary-Lou felt slightly sick.

Then Darrell spoilt it all! She passed by with her mother and father, and Mrs. Lacey was struck by her good looks and happy smile.

"*There's* a nice girl, dear!" she said to Gwendoline. "Is she one of your friends? Let us speak to her."

"Oh, no, she's not a friend of mine," began Gwendoline, but Mary-Lou, delighted at this praise of Darrell, was calling to her. "Darrell! Darrell! Mrs. Lacey wants to speak to you."

Darrell went over to Mrs. Lacey and was introduced by a glowering Gwendoline. "And are you going to go in for the swimming-sports?" asked Mrs. Lacey, graciously. "I hear dear Gwendoline is not, bless her."

"Gwendoline! Oh, she can't swim a stroke!" said Darrell. "We always yell at her because she takes five minutes putting one toe into the water. Don't we, Gwendoline?"

This was all said in good humour and fun – but Gwendoline could willingly have pushed Darrell over the cliff at that moment! She went very red.

Mrs. Lacey really thought that Darrell was joking. She laughed the tinkling laugh which she thought was so pretty. "I suppose if Gwendoline entered she'd beat you all!" she said. "As she does at tennis – and lessons, I suppose."

Darrell looked in astonishment at Gwendoline, who was glaring at her, crimson in the face. "Gwendoline's been stuffing you up, I expect!" she said with a laugh, and went off to join her own party.

"What a very outspoken, blunt sort of girl," said Miss Winter, puzzled and worried.

Gwendoline recovered herself. "Oh, she's not a nice girl," she said. "Nobody likes her. She hasn't got any friend of her own at all – and you can see why. She's always running other people down. Jealous, I suppose. Don't you take any notice of her, Mother. Mary-Lou here will tell you I'm first-rate at tennis and the rest!"

But that was beyond even timid Mary-Lou! She just looked more scared than ever, and murmured something about going to speak to Mam'zelle – and off she went, glad to escape from the Lacey family for a few minutes.

On the way to the car, after Darrell had shown her parents every single thing she could think of, from the view up in North Tower, to the inside of her very well-tidied desk, the Rivers' family saw Sally Hope.

"Why, isn't that Sally Hope?" said Mrs. Rivers, stopping. "I'm sure it is. There was a very good photograph of her in her mother's drawing-room, when I went to tea there the other day."

"Yes. That's Sally," said Darrell. "Do you want to speak to her, Mother?"

"Well, I have a message for her from her mother," said Mrs. Rivers. So Darrell raised her clear voice and called. "Sally! Sally Hope! Come here a minute, will you?"

Sally must have heard Darrell, for everyone around did. But if so, she took no notice at all. She plunged down into a path that led through some bushes in the drive and disappeared.

"Blow her!" said Darrell. "I should have thought she would have heard my yell. I asked her to come out with us, Mother, but she wouldn't."

"Come along," said her father, opening the door of

the car. "We'll go along the cliff and then take an exciting road I've found that leads right down to a lonely little cove. We'll have our lunch there."

Darrell and Emily got in. Emily was enjoying herself. Mrs. Rivers was so nice, and asked her so many questions about herself. Usually people found Emily dull, and left her alone. But Mrs. Rivers, thinking that Emily was Darrell's chosen friend, was very anxious to know her well.

She soon learnt that Emily was very fond of sewing. Darrell listened to her chattering in astonishment. She had never heard Emily talk so much before! Gracious, hark at her describing the cushion-cover she was making – the colours, the stitches and everything!

"It's always been a disappointment to me that Darrell never took any interest in embroidery," said Mrs. Rivers to Emily. "I'm very fond of it too. I've done the seats of six of our chairs at home, in tapestry work."

"Oh, *have* you!" exclaimed Emily. "I've done some too – but only two so far. I loved that work."

"Perhaps you will be able to interest Darrell in sewing!" said Mrs. Rivers, laughing. "It's as much as I can do at home to get her to do a simple darn!"

"Well, I'll teach Darrell to darn, if she likes," said Emily, eager to please this nice Mrs. Rivers.

Darrell was horrified. Gracious, she hadn't brought Emily out to have her planning with her mother to teach her darning! She changed the subject at once, and told them about Gwendoline and how she had been boasting to her mother and governess.

Soon they were down on the beach, eating the most gorgeous lunch Darrell had had that term. Cold chicken and pickles – *pickles*! There was never a pickle to be seen at school. Little cardboard containers full of fresh salad and mayonnaise sauce. Delicious! Jam-tarts and slabs of chocolate ice-cream. What a lunch!

"And ginger-beer to wash it down," said Mrs. Rivers,

filling up the glasses. "More chicken, Darrell? There's plenty."

After lunch it was time to go back for the sports. Emily was not in the swimming, so she said she would find Darrell's parents good places to watch from. Darrell left them in her care when she got back to Malory Towers to change.

It was such a happy day. Everyone seemed in a good temper, and jokes flew about everywhere. Even the two Mam'zelles went about arm-in-arm, a thing that they had not done at all that term.

The swimming-sports were exciting. Mrs. Rivers was delighted with Darrell's strong swimming, graceful diving, and fearlessness. She was one of the best of the small girls. Some of the big girls were extremely clever in their diving, especially Marilyn, the sixth-form games-captain. Everyone cheered her as she did a graceful swallow-dive from the topmost board.

"And can you do all these things, darling?" Darrell heard Mrs. Lacey ask Gwendoline. Gwendoline, who was near Darrell and a few others, looked round warily, wishing her mother wouldn't ask such awkward questions in public.

"Well – not quite all," she said, and Miss Winter patted her fondly on the shoulder.

"Always so modest," she said, and Darrell could hardly stop herself laughing outright at the thought of Gwendoline being called modest. She looked scornfully at little Mary-Lou sitting near Gwendoline, wondering how she could possibly listen to all the bigger girl's boasting and yet say nothing.

At tea-time Darrell and Emily kept the plates of the grown-ups (and their own!) well supplied with strawberries and cream, and fetched ice-creams in plenty. What a lunch they had had – and now, what a tea! Besides the strawberries and ice-creams, there were little buns and cakes and biscuits of every kind. Malory

Towers knew how to do things well!

"Mother! There's Sally Hope again!" said Darrell suddenly, catching sight of Sally's head in the distance. "I'll get her in a minute. By the way, you never told me how that mistake about Sally's baby sister happened – the one you said she had got, and hasn't."

"But Darrell dear – she *has* got a baby sister!" said her mother in surprise. "I've seen her!"

"Well – whatever *does* Sally mean!" said Darrell. "I really must get her and find out!"

A Sudden Quarrel

But Sally was not easy to find. She seemed to have completely disappeared again. It occurred to Darrell to wonder if Sally was avoiding her – but no, why should she? There would be no reason for that.

She hunted everywhere for Sally. Nobody knew where she was. It was peculiar. Darrell went back to her parents, anxious not to lose any more of their company, for time was precious now.

"Well, *I* can't find Sally," she said. "She's completely vanished. Anyway, I'll give her her mother's message. What was it, Mother?"

"Oh, her mother seemed a little worried about Sally, because it's her first term at boarding school, and Sally writes such funny wooden little letters," said Mrs. Rivers. "I showed Mrs. Hope some of *your* letters, darling. I knew you wouldn't mind; and she said she did wish Sally would write more news to her, and send her letters like yours. She said she seemed to have lost touch with her completely. She was really very worried. She wanted me to speak to Sally and tell her she sent her fondest love, and was so sorry she couldn't come and see her this half-term. And she said her baby sister sent her hugs and kisses."

"I'll tell her," said Darrell, very puzzled. "But Mother dear, Sally's awfully funny about things. She truly and honestly did tell me she hadn't got a sister, and she was furious with me for talking about her mother. She said I was interfering and all sorts of things."

"Well – perhaps she was joking," said Mrs. Rivers, also rather puzzled. "Sally *does* know she's got a baby sister at home. For one thing, that was why she was sent to boarding school, so that the baby, who is rather delicate, could have all Mrs. Hope's care. It's a dear little thing."

"Been losing your temper yet?" asked Darrell's father, with a twinkle in his eye. Darrell went red.

"Well – I did once," she said. "And after I'd made up my mind I wouldn't, too!"

"Oh, Darrell – you didn't lose it badly, I hope," said her mother, anxiously.

Emily answered for Darrell. "Oh, she just gave a most exasperating girl some jolly good slaps in the pool! You could almost hear them up at the Towers!"

"*Darrell!*" said her mother, shocked. Darrell grinned. "I know. Awful of me, wasn't it? I shan't do it again. I've got my temper well in hand now."

"We've all *wanted* to do a bit of slapping where that particular girl is concerned," said Emily, "so secretly we were rather pleased!"

They all laughed. Darrell felt so happy that she was sure she would never lose her temper again in her life! What a pity a day like this had to come to an end!

But it did come to an end. At about six o'clock the cars began to purr out of the big drive, and girls waved wildly. One by one their parents went, and the excited chattering died down. The girls went into their common rooms to talk over the events of the day.

100

After a while Darrell remembered the message she had for Sally Hope. She glanced round the common room. Sally wasn't there. Where was she? She seemed always to be disappearing!

"Where's Sally Hope?" asked Darrell.

"I believe she's in one of the music-rooms," said Katherine. "Goodness knows why she wants to practise today, when everyone is let off lessons!"

"I'll go and find her," said Darrell, and walked off. She made her way to the music-rooms, where the girls did their practising each day. They were tiny rooms, containing only a piano, a stool, and a chair.

Music came from two of them. Darrell peeped into the first one. Irene was there, playing softly to herself. She didn't even see Darrell. Darrell smiled and shut the door. Irene was certainly mad on music!

She came to the other practice room, from which music was coming. It was not the entrancing melodies that Irene had been playing, though, but plain five-finger exercises, played over and over again, over and over again, in an almost angry manner.

Darrell opened the door. Yes – Sally was there all right. Good. Darrell went in and shut the door. Sally turned round and scowled.

"I'm practising," she said. "Get out."

"What's the matter with you?" said Darrell, feeling annoyed immediately. "You don't need to jump down my throat like that. I've been trying to find you all day. My mother wanted to speak to you."

"Well, I didn't want to speak to her," said Sally, and began to thump out the irritating exercise again, up and down, up and down.

"*Why* shouldn't you want to speak to my mother?" cried Darrell, angrily. "She had a message for you from *your* mother."

No answer. Up and down, up and down went Sally's

fingers on the notes, more loudly than ever. Darrell lost her temper.

"Stop playing!" she shouted. "Don't be so horribly rude! Whatever's the matter with you!"

Sally put the loud pedal down and crashed the notes more loudly than ever. Plainly she was not going to listen to a word.

Darrell went near to her and put her mouth to her ear.

"Why did you say you haven't got a sister? You *have*, and that's why your mother couldn't come and see you! But she sent you her love and said . . ."

Sally swung round from the piano, her face looking queer and white. "Shut up!" she said. "Interfering little busybody! Leave me alone. Just because you've been with your mother all day long, and had her fussing round you, you think you can come and taunt me like this! I hate you!"

"You're mad!" cried Darrell, and she struck her hand on the piano, making a queer sound of crashing notes. "You won't listen when I want to tell you things. But you *shall* listen! Your mother told mine that you only write her funny wooden letters. . . . She said . . ."

"I *won't* listen!" said Sally, in a choking voice, and got up from the stool. She pushed Darrell blindly away. But Darrell could not bear to be touched when she was in a temper, and she shoved back with all her might. She was strong, and she sent Sally flying across the little room. She fell across the chair, and lay there for a moment.

She put her hand on her stomach. "Oh, it hurts," she said. "Oh, you wicked girl, Darrell!"

Darrell was still trembling with anger as Sally stumbled out of the room. But almost immediately her rage went, and she was overwhelmed with horror. How *could* she have been so awful? Sally was queer and silly and horrid, it was true – but she, Darrell, had used

She sent Sally flying

her strength against her to hurt her. She had lost her temper all over again, after boasting to her parents only a little while ago that she never would any more.

She ran to the door, eager to go after Sally and beg her pardon. But Sally was nowhere to be seen. Darrell ran back to the common room. No Sally there, either. She sat down in a chair and rubbed her hot forehead. What a scene! How disgusting! *Why* couldn't she manage her temper?

"What's up?" asked Alicia.

"Oh – nothing much. Sally was a bit difficult, that's all – and I lost my temper," said Darrell.

"Idiot!" said Alicia. "What did you do? Slap her? Give her some broth without any bread?"

Darrell couldn't smile. She felt near tears. What a horrid ending to such a lovely day! After all the excitement, and now this sudden row, she felt quite exhausted. She was not at all pleased when Emily came up with her sewing.

"I do think your people are nice," began Emily, and started to chatter in a way she seldom did. How boring! Darrell wanted to tell Emily to be quiet. If she had been Alicia she would – but as a rule she was kinder than the sharp-tongued Alicia, and did not like to hurt people's feelings. So she bore with Emily as patiently as she could.

Mary-Lou watched her from the other side of the room. She wanted to come over and join Emily and Darrell. But Gwendoline was pouring out reams of family history to her, and she had to listen. Also she was a little afraid that Darrell might snub her if she went across.

Darrell watched for Sally to appear in the common room. Perhaps she could slip over to her then and tell her she was sorry. She was ashamed of herself now, and she could only put it right by telling Sally. Oh, dear! It was awful to have a temper that simply rose up out of the blue, before you even knew it was coming! What *could* you do with a temper like that?

Sally didn't come back to the common room. Soon the supper-bell went and the girls filed into the dining-room. Darrell looked for Sally again. But still she wasn't there. This was really very queer.

Miss Potts noticed that there was an empty chair. "Who's missing?" she said.

"Sally Hope," said Darrell. "I last saw her in one of the practice rooms – about an hour ago."

"Well, go and fetch her," said Miss Potts, impatiently.

"Oh, she left when I was there," said Darrell. "I don't know where she went to."

"We'll get on without her then," said Miss Potts. "She must have heard the supper-bell."

The girls chattered about the day they had had. Only Darrell was silent. Was Sally somewhere, very upset? What could be the matter with her? Why was she so queer about things? Was she unhappy about something?

Mary-Lou sniffed loudly. "Where's your hanky?" asked Miss Potts. "Haven't you got one? Oh, Mary-Lou, you know you must always have one. Go and get one at once. I can't bear that sniff of yours."

Mary-Lou slipped out of the room, and ran up to the dormy. She didn't come back for a little while and Miss Potts became impatient.

"Really! It seems to take Mary-Lou all evening to find a hanky!"

There came the sound of running steps and the door of the dining-room was flung open. Mary-Lou came in, looking even more scared than usual.

"Miss Potts! Oh, Miss Potts! I've found Sally. She's lying on her bed in the dormy, and she's making an awful noise!"

"What sort of noise?" said Miss Potts, hurriedly getting up.

"A groaning sort of noise and she keeps holding herself and saying, 'Oh, my tummy!'" said poor Mary-Lou, bursting into tears. "Oh, Miss Potts, do go to her. She wouldn't even speak to me!"

"Girls, get on with your supper," said Miss Potts, briskly. "It sounds as if Sally has eaten too many strawberries and too much ice-cream. Katherine, go and tell Matron, please, and ask her to go up to your dormy."

She swept out of the room. The girls began talking at once, asking scared Mary-Lou all kinds of questions. Only Darrell still sat silent, a cold fear creeping round her heart.

She had flung Sally across the room, and Sally had fallen over that chair! She must have hurt herself in the stomach then. Darrell remembered how she had said, "It hurts." It wasn't too many strawberries and too much ice-cream. It was Darrell's temper that had caused the trouble!

Darrell couldn't eat any more supper. She slipped off to the common room to be by herself. Surely Sally wasn't *much* hurt? Just bruised, perhaps. Surely Miss Potts would come in soon and say cheerfully, "Well, well! Nothing much wrong with Sally after all!"

"Oh, I hope she does, I hope she does," said poor Darrell, and waited impatiently and anxiously for the sound of Miss Potts's quick footsteps.

A Bad Time for Darrell

The girls poured into the common room after their supper. They had half an hour before bedtime. They were tired after their exciting day, and some of them were sleepy already.

Alicia looked at Darrell in surprise. "Why so gloomy?" she said.

"Well – I was just wondering about Sally," said Darrell. "Hoping she wasn't very ill."

"Why ever should she be?" said Alicia. "Lots of people can't eat strawberries without getting a pain or a rash. One of my brothers is like that."

Alicia plunged into one of her bits of family history and Darrell listened gratefully. Alicia did not relate stories that glorified herself, as Gwendoline always did – she simply poured out amusing tales of the life she and her brothers led in the holidays at home – and, if Alicia was to be believed, the pranks they got up to were enough to turn any mother's hair completely grey! However, Alicia's mother had not seemed to Darrell to have any grey hairs at all, when she had seen her that day.

The bed-time bell went for the first- and second-formers. They put away their things at once. Matron did not show much patience with laggards at bed-time. There were too many girls to hustle into bed for that!

Miss Potts had not come back. Darrell felt her anxiety creeping over her again. Perhaps Matron would know. She would ask her about Sally as soon as she saw her hovering around the bathrooms.

But Matron wasn't there. Mam'zelle was there instead, beaming placidly at everyone, still in a good temper because of the lovely day they had all had.

"Hallo, Mam'zelle! Where's Matron?" asked Alicia in surprise.

"Looking after Sally Hope," said Mam'zelle. "Ah, the poor child – she is in great pain."

Darrell's heart sank. "Is she – is she in the San. then?" she asked. Girls who were ill were always put in the San., which consisted of a good many nice rooms above the Head Mistress's own suite of rooms. There was also a special matron for the San. itself, a smiling, but strict hospital nurse, who was extremely efficient not only at dealing with any kind of school accident or illness, but also at dealing with any kind of girl!

"Yes. Of course she is in the San. She is very ill," said Mam'zelle. Then, with her love of exaggerating, she added a sentence or two that sent Darrell's heart down into her boots. "It is her poor tommy – no, tummy is what you say, *n'est ce pas*? She has a big pain there."

"Oh," said Darrell. "Do they – do they know what has caused the pain, Mam'zelle? Has Sally hurt herself?"

Mam'zelle didn't know. "All I know is that it is not the strawberries and the ice-cream," she said. "Because Sally did not have any. She has told Matron that."

That made it all the more certain, then, that it must have been Darrell's rough push and the fall that followed! Poor Darrell! She felt so miserable that Mam'zelle's sharp eyes noticed her downcast face and she began to wonder if here was another girl about to be ill!

"You feel all right, my little Darrell?" she said, in a sympathetic voice.

"Oh, yes, thank you," said Darrell, startled. "I'm just – well, just tired, I suppose."

Darrell hardly slept at all that night. She was so horrified at what had happened. How could she have lost her temper so thoroughly, how could she have yelled at Sally like that and how *could* she have sent her flying across the room? She, Darrell, was wicked! It was true that Sally was queer and annoying, but that was no excuse for Darrell's behaviour.

Now Sally was ill and in pain. Had she said anything about Darrell losing her temper? Darrell felt herself growing cold as she thought of what Miss Grayling might do if she heard.

"She would hear about my slapping Gwendoline too, and she would send for me and tell me I was a failure already," thought Darrell. "Oh, Sally, Sally, do get better by tomorrow! Then I'll tell you I'm terribly sorry, and I'll try to make it up to you all I can."

She fell asleep at last, and was very tired when the dressing-bell rang for them all to get up. Her first thought was Sally. She saw the girl's empty bed and shivered. How she hoped Sally would be back there that night!

She ran downstairs before any one else. She saw Miss Potts and went to her. "Please," she said, "how is Sally?"

Miss Potts thought what a kind child Darrell was. "She's not at all well, I'm afraid," she said. "The doctor is still doubtful about what exactly is the matter. But she really seems rather ill, poor child. It was so sudden, too – she seemed all right yesterday."

Darrell turned away, miserable. Yes, Sally had been all right till she had fallen across that chair. *She* knew what was the matter – but nobody else did! It was plain that Sally hadn't told anyone of the quarrel.

It was Sunday. Darrell prayed hard for Sally all the time she was in church. She felt very guilty and ashamed. She also felt very much afraid. She felt that she ought to tell Miss Potts or Matron about the quarrel and how she had flung poor Sally across the room – but she was too frightened to tell!

Too frightened! Darrell was so fearless in the usual way that it was something strange and queer to her to feel afraid. But she *was* afraid. Supposing Sally was very *very* ill! Supposing – just supposing she didn't get better! Supposing Darrell's temper caused all that!

She couldn't, couldn't tell anyone, because they would think her so wicked, and she would disgrace her mother and father. People would say "That's the girl whose temper caused her to be expelled from Malory Towers! You know she made another girl terribly ill!"

It would be awful to be sent away from Malory Towers in disgrace. She would never get over it. But she was sure Miss Grayling wouldn't keep her another day if she knew that she had caused Sally's illness and pain.

"I can't tell anyone, I can't!" thought poor Darrell. "I'm afraid of letting people know, because of what would happen to me, and how it would make Mother and Daddy feel. I'm a coward, but I daren't tell. I never knew I was a coward before!"

She suddenly thought of Mary-Lou, whom she had so often called a coward. Poor Mary-Lou – now she knew how *she* felt when she was afraid of something. It was a horrible feeling. You couldn't get away from it. How *could* she have sneered at Mary-Lou and taunted her? It was bad enough to feel afraid of something without being taunted about it.

Darrell felt very sad and very humble. She had started the term in such high hopes and spirits. She was going to be top! She was going to shine in everything and make her parents proud of her! She was going to find a fine girl for a friend. And she hadn't done any of those things.

She had got a low place in the form. She hadn't found herself a friend. She had been hateful to little Mary-Lou who had so shyly and eagerly offered her friendship – and now she had done something wicked and didn't dare to say anything about it!

Darrell was certainly down in the dumps that day and nobody could rouse her out of them. Miss Potts wondered if she was sickening for something and kept a sharp eye on her. Mary-Lou was worried, and hovered round hoping to be able to do something. And for once Darrell was kind to her and did not snap at her to send her away. She felt grateful for Mary-Lou's liking and sympathy.

Two doctors came to see Sally that day! The news went round North Tower House. "She's *fearfully* ill! But it's nothing infectious so we're not in quarantine.

110

Poor Sally. Tessie says she had to go and see the Head this morning and she heard Sally groaning in the San. rooms above!"

How Darrell wished her mother was there that day! But she couldn't remember where her parents had gone to, though they had told her. She had forgotten in the excitement of yesterday. She sat down in a rocky corner by the sea, and thought things out.

She couldn't be a coward any longer, because it would be worse to stay at Malory Towers and know she was a coward than it would be to leave, knowing she had been brave enough to own up. But whom should she tell?

"I'd better write and tell Sally's mother," she thought. "She's the one that's nearest to Sally. I'll write and tell her all about the quarrel, and how it happened and everything. I'll have to tell her, too, how Sally says she hasn't got a sister. That's all very queer, but maybe Mrs. Hope will understand it. Then Mrs. Hope can do what she likes — tell the Head, I expect! Oh, dear! But I shall feel better when it's done."

She left her seat by the sea and went back to North Tower. She got out her writing pad and began to write. It was not an easy letter to compose, but Darrell always found writing easy, and she poured out everything to Mrs. Hope — about the quarrel and what led up to it, and all about Sally not wanting to speak to Mrs. Rivers, and how unhappy she seemed to be. She was quite surprised to find how much she seemed to know about Sally!

She felt better immediately she had finished the letter. She didn't read it through, but stuck a stamp on the envelope and posted it at once. Mrs. Hope would get it the very next morning!

Then another rumour ran through North Tower. "Sally's taken a turn for the worse! A specialist is coming to see her! Her people have been telegraphed for! They're coming tomorrow!"

Darrell could not eat anything at all that day. It was the longest day she had ever known. Mary-Lou, scared by Darrell's stricken face, kept close by her – and Darrell welcomed her and felt comforted. Mary-Lou had no idea why Darrell looked so miserable, and didn't dare to ask her. She forgot the many sneers and taunts that Darrell had thrown at her for her weakness and feebleness; she only wanted to help.

The other girls did not notice anything much. They went for walks, bathed, lay about in the sun, and had a happy, lazy Sunday. Miss Potts still kept an eye on Darrell. What *could* be the matter with her? Was it Sally's illness that was worrying her? No, it couldn't be. She hadn't been at all friendly with Sally. Nobody had, for that matter.

Bed-time came at last. Matron had no more news of Sally, except that she was no better. No one was allowed to see her, of course. Matron had been quite shocked because Darrell had begged to go and see her for a moment or two!

Darrell lay in bed, thinking. The third- and fourth-formers came up to bed. The fifth-formers came and then the sixth. Then Matron, Mam'zelle and Miss Potts retired too, and Darrell heard lights clicking out. It was late. It was dark outside. Everyone was asleep except Darrell.

"I simply can't lie here thinking and thinking!" said Darrell to herself desperately, and she flung off her covers. "I shall go mad! I shall get up and go into the Court! The roses will smell sweet there, and I shall get cool and perhaps be able to go to sleep!"

She slipped on her dressing-gown and went quietly out of the room. Nobody stirred. She crept down the wide stairs and out into the Court. And then, in the stillness of the night, she heard the sound of a car purring

up the hill to Malory Towers! It stopped outside. Whoever could it be, so late at night?

Darrell glanced up at the windows of the San. There
were bright lights there. Sally couldn't be asleep, or the
lights would be dimmed. What was going on now?
Oh dear, if only she knew!

Darrell slipped through the archway that led from
the Court to the drive. Yes, a car stood there, a dark
shape, silent now and empty. Whoever had come in it
had gone into Malory Towers. Darrell crept round to
the door that led into the Head's building. Someone
had left it open! She pushed it and went inside. Now she
would find out what was happening!

A Wonderful Surprise

There was a little light burning in the hall. The Head
Mistress's rooms were in darkness. She was evidently
upstairs in the San. Darrell crept upstairs. There were
bright lights everywhere, and a good deal of bustle.
What was happening to poor Sally?

Darrell couldn't understand what was going on.
Sally must be very ill to have so many people bothering
about her like this in the middle of the night! Darrell's
heart felt very heavy. She didn't dare to go any farther
in case someone saw her. But she felt she *must* stay
where she was. She must get to know *some*thing! She
couldn't possibly go back to bed without finding out
what was happening. If only, only she could help!

She sat down on a window-seat, and drew the heavy
curtains round her, straining her ears to catch a word
from any of the people bustling about from one of the
San. rooms to another. That was Matron's voice – the
matron of North Tower! And that was the other
Matron's voice, very crisp and sharp, giving an order.

And that was a man's voice. Darrell held her breath and listened to the mysterious voices and noises, but she couldn't hear a word.

Oh, what would they all say if they knew that she, hot-tempered, wicked little Darrell was at the bottom of all this fuss and worry and bother? Darrell pulled the curtain round her head and wept great tears that soaked into the heavy silk.

She sat there for about half an hour. Then, quite suddenly, and without meaning to, she fell fast asleep! Lost in the heavy curtains, she slept, tired out.

She did not know how long she slept. She awoke again later, hearing noises. She sat up, wondering where in the wide world she was! Then she remembered. Of course – she was near the San. She had come to find out what was happening to Sally.

At once all the fear and anxiety closed round her once again. She felt lonely and lost, and wanted her mother. She clutched the curtains round her as she heard voices coming near. Was it doctors? Nurses? Perhaps the Head Mistress herself?

And then Darrell's heart almost stopped beating! Someone was going by the window-seat where she sat, someone who spoke in a voice she knew and loved!

"She'll be all right," said the voice. "Just got her nicely in time! Now . . ."

Darrell sat as if she was turned to stone, listening to that well-known voice! It couldn't be! It couldn't be! It *couldn't be* her own father's voice!

She suddenly found herself able to move. She thrust the curtains aside and looked between them. She saw her father walking along with the Matron, talking earnestly. Yes, it was, it really was her father.

"Daddy!" squealed Darrell, forgetting absolutely everything except the fact that there was her father, whom she thought was miles away, walking along the

114

She thrust the curtain aside and looked through

passage just near her. "Daddy! Oh, Daddy! Stop, here's Darrell!"

Her father stopped as if he was shot! He couldn't believe his ears! Darrell leapt down from the window-seat and flung herself on him like a small thunderbolt. She clung to him and began to cry.

"What's the matter, darling?" said her father, amazed. "Why are you here?"

Miss Grayling came up, astonished and rather disapproving. "Darrell! What are you here for, child? Mr. Rivers, you had better come into my room downstairs, please."

Carrying Darrell in his arms, her father followed Miss Grayling downstairs, with Matron clucking behind like an astonished hen. Darrell clung to her father as if she would never let him go. Was she dreaming? Could it be that this was really her own father, in the middle of the night? Darrell couldn't imagine how or why he was there, but it was enough that he was.

He sat down in a big armchair with Darrell on his knees. Matron disappeared. Only Miss Grayling was there, and she looked in a very puzzled manner at Darrell and her father. There was something here she didn't understand.

"You cry all you want to, then tell me what's the matter," said Darrell's father. "Why, we only saw you yesterday, and you were so happy! Never mind, I'm here, and I'll put everything right for you."

"You can't!" wept Darrell. "I've been wicked! It was my temper again. Oh, Daddy, it's all *my* fault that Sally is so ill!"

"My dear child, what *are* you talking about?" said her father, puzzled. Darrell snuggled her head into his chest and began to feel much better. Daddy could always put things right. So could Mother. What a blessing he was here tonight.

116

Then she raised her head, and spoke in surprise. "But Daddy – *why* are you here? I thought you were miles away!"

"Well, I was," said Mr. Rivers. "But Miss Grayling telephoned to me to say that little Sally Hope had appendicitis and the surgeon they usually had was ill, so could I come straight along and do the operation. So of course I did! I hopped into the car, drove here, found everything ready, did the little operation, and here I am! And Sally will be quite all right and back again in school in about two weeks' time!"

A great load fell away from Darrell's heart. She could almost feel it rolling away. Why, appendicitis was something *any*one might have! Her father was always curing appendicitis! She spoke anxiously.

"Daddy – appendicitis couldn't be caused by a push – or a fall – could it?"

"Good gracious, no!" said her father. "Sally's had this little affair coming on for some time, there's no doubt about that. All the term and before that, I should think. But what makes you ask that question?"

Then everything came pouring out – how funny and queer and rude Sally had been – how Darrell had lost her temper – the violent push, the fall – everything!

"And I worried and worried and worried," said Darrell, with a sob. "I thought if Miss Grayling knew, she would send me away from Malory Towers, and you and Mother would be ashamed of me, and I couldn't sleep, so I got up and . . ."

"What a silly little girl!" said her father, and kissed the top of her head. "Perhaps we had better take you away from Malory Towers ourselves, and have you at home, if you are going to think such silly things, Darrell!"

"Oh, no – don't do that! I love being here!" said Darrell. "Oh, Daddy – if you *knew* how different I

117

feel now that I know Sally was going to be ill, anyhow – it wasn't anything to do with me, after all. But oh, dear – I wrote to Mrs. Hope about it! What *will* she think?"

Then she had to tell all about the letter and what she had said. Her father and Miss Grayling were puzzled to hear how Sally had said she hadn't a baby sister.

"Something queer there that must be sorted out," said Mr. Rivers to Miss Grayling. "Might prevent her from getting better as quickly as she ought to. When did you say Mr. and Mrs. Hope were coming?"

"Tomorrow," said Miss Grayling. "I'll see them and explain. Now, Mr. Rivers – would you like us to give you a bed here tonight? It's so late."

"Oh, no!" said Mr. Rivers. "I'm used to driving out late at night. I'll go back, thank you. And Darrell must go to bed. Now don't worry any more, darling – things are all right – and your little push didn't do Sally any harm, though probably the fall made her feel her bad tummy a little bit more. I expect she felt ill all day, poor child."

"It wasn't a little push I gave her. It was a big one," said Darrell.

"It makes me sad to think I've handed on to you the temper I've got myself," said her father. Darrell tightened her arms round his neck.

"Don't worry. I'll get on top of it!" she said. "I'll soon do what you do – keep it for worth-while things!"

"Well, good night, darling," said her father, and kissed her. "Go and see Sally as soon as you're allowed to. I think you'll feel better then!"

"I feel better now!" said Darrell, and slipped off his knee. Her eyes were red but she was smiling. How different she felt! All her worry was gone.

Her father went off in the darkness in his car. Miss Grayling herself took Darrell to bed and tucked her in. Darrell fell asleep even before the Head Mistress was out of the room.

And, in the San. Sally slept too, her pain gone. Matron watched over her, pleased to hear her steady, regular breathing. What a deft, quick surgeon Darrell's father was – only thirteen minutes to do the operation! Matron thought how lucky it was that he had been near enough to come.

Next morning dawned fair and bright. Darrell awoke when the dressing-bell went, tired but happy again. She lay and thought for half a minute. Her heart was full of thankfulness. Sally would be all right. Her father had said so. And he had said that Darrell hadn't had anything to do with her illness. All her worry had been for nothing. No – not quite for nothing. It had made a deep impression on her. It wouldn't be nearly so difficult to keep her temper next time. She had had a jolly good lesson!

"I wish I could do something to show I'm grateful and thankful it's all turned out like this," thought Darrell, jumping out of bed. "But there's nothing I can do. I wonder how Sally is today."

Sally was getting on very well indeed. When she heard that her mother and father were coming to see her she could hardly believe her ears.

"But is *Mother* coming?" she asked, time and again. "Are you sure *Mother's* coming? But she couldn't come last Saturday. Is she really coming?"

Miss Grayling received Mr. and Mrs. Hope in her big drawing-room. Mr. Hope was a big burly man, looking anxious. Mrs. Hope was a delicate-looking woman with a sweet face.

"Sally is not quite ready for you to see her yet," said Miss Grayling. "I am so glad to be able to tell you that the operation was very successful and she is getting along wonderfully well. Mr. Rivers, the surgeon, happened to be at a hotel not far off, and we got him to do it. He is the father of one of our girls here, Darrell Rivers."

"Oh – Darrell Rivers," said Mrs. Hope, and she took out a letter from her bag. "I had such a *queer* letter from her today, Miss Grayling. Please read it. She appears to think she was the cause of Sally's illness, but of course she wasn't. But the other things she says are very worrying to me. Could we have Darrell in to speak to us, before I see Sally, do you think?"

Miss Grayling read the letter and looked grave. "There *is* something puzzling here," she said. "Why should Sally keep saying she has no sister, when she knows she has?"

"I don't know," said Mrs. Hope, sadly. "But Sally has been queer ever since Baby Daphne came. She won't look at her or speak to her – and once, when she didn't know I was looking, I saw her pinch poor Daphne cruelly. And Sally is not a cruel child."

"Have you any other children?" asked Miss Grayling. Mrs. Hope shook her head.

"No," she said. "Sally was twelve when Daphne was born. She had been the only child for all that time. I thought she would be so pleased to have a sister. We haven't spoilt Sally, you know – but she didn't have to share us with anyone till Daphne came – and sometimes I wondered if she was – well – jealous."

"Of course she was!" said Miss Grayling at once. "I should think, Mrs. Hope, that Sally is very much attached to you, and resented sharing your love when the baby came. She probably didn't like to tell you so, in case you thought badly of her."

"Oh, she never said a word to me!" said Mrs. Hope. "She just changed, that's all. She wasn't merry and gay any more, she didn't come to us and love us as she used to do, and she seemed to hate the baby. I thought it would blow over. And then, when it didn't, I and my husband thought it would be best if Sally came to boarding school, because I wasn't very well at the time, and it was all I could do to look after the baby, without having to cope with Sally too. We did it for the best."

"Yes, I see," said Miss Grayling, thoughtfully. "But, from Sally's point of view it must have seemed that you didn't want her any more, but had sent her away to make room for a baby who was taking up all your care and attention. Mrs. Hope, this jealousy of a much younger child is very common and very natural, and you mustn't blame Sally for it. Neither must you let it grow. If only you can make Sally feel you love her as much as ever you did it will be quite all right. Now — shall we have Darrell in?"

Darrell was sent for. She came in nervously, scared of what Mrs. Hope might say. But she was soon put at her ease, and she told all she knew.

Miss Grayling turned to Mrs. Hope. "I think it would be a good idea if we let Darrell go in to see Sally for a few minutes before you do," she said. "We will let her tell Sally that you have come — and we will let her say that you have left the baby behind in order to hurry as fast as possible to Sally. Will you do that, Darrell?"

Darrell nodded. She had suddenly seen all Sally's trouble! Why, she was jealous of her little baby sister! So jealous that she wouldn't even admit she had got one. Poor, funny Sally. It was so lovely to have a sister. Sally didn't know how lucky she was!

"I'll tell her," she said, eagerly. "I'll do what I can too, when you've gone, to make Sally think it's fun to have a sister. I wanted to do *some*thing — and I shall love to do that!"

Darrell went to the San. upstairs. She had a little note with her for Matron from Miss Grayling. "Please allow Darrell to see Sally for a few minutes before her mother comes."

Matron, surprised and not very pleased, opened the door to let Darrell in. Darrell tiptoed in. It was a pleasant room, with three white beds in it, and a lovely view from the big windows. Everything was creamy white and spotlessly clean. In the end bed lay Sally, white but bright-eyed.

"Hallo, Sally," said Darrell. "I've been so worried about you. Are you better? Did my father make you better?"

"Yes. I do like him. He was so kind," said Sally. "I did feel so awful all Saturday, Darrell. But I couldn't tell anyone, could I? I couldn't spoil the day."

"I think you're very brave," said Darrell. "I say – guess who's here to see you?"

"Not my mother?" said Sally, her eyes shining. Darrell nodded. "Yes. And your father too. And do you know, Sally, your mother has left behind your little baby sister, so that she could come more quickly to see you? Fancy that! She must think an awful lot of you, because usually mothers can't bear to leave babies when they're small."

Sally seemed to have forgotten that she had told Darrell she had no sister. She reached out for Darrell's hand. "Hasn't she brought Baby?" she whispered. "Did she leave her behind? Really and truly?"

"Yes, poor little thing," said Darrell. "She must be feeling lonely! I've got a little sister, too. It's lovely

122

to have a sister. Mine looks up to me no end and thinks I'm wonderful. I expect yours will, too."

Sally's ideas of sisters underwent a sudden change. Things seemed suddenly to fall into their proper places. She smiled gratefully at Darrell. "You'll come and see me when you can, won't you?" she said. "And don't say anything about – about – all my silliness, will you? To the others, I mean."

"Of course not. It wasn't silliness. It was just a mistake on your part," said Darrell. "Why, anyone could see by giving one look at your mother that she's a *proper* mother – I mean the kind that would always love you, however many children she had, or whatever you did. I think she's a darling."

"So do I," said Sally, with a sigh. "I'm sorry I was such a beast to you, Darrell."

"And I can't tell you *how* sorry I am for having shoved you like that when you had such a pain in your tummy," said Darrell.

"Did you shove me?" said Sally. "I've forgotten. Look, what's Matron saying?"

Matron was beckoning for Darrell to come away. Mr. and Mrs. Hope were outside the door. Darrell said a hurried good-bye and tiptoed out. Mr. and Mrs. Hope went in, and Darrell heard Sally's low cry of joy as she saw her mother.

Darrell skipped happily down the stairs and through the hall into the Court. She ran to the building in which her own classroom was. The bell was just going for the ending of a lesson.

Darrell slipped into the first-form classroom. The girls looked up at her.

"Where *have* you been? You've been ages! You've missed half of maths., lucky pig."

"I've been to see Sally," said Darrell, importantly.

"Fibber! No one is allowed to see her yet," said Irene.

"Well, I *have*. And she says my father has cured her pain and made her much better," said Darrell, proud to have such a father. "He came in the night. I saw him."

"Darrell Rivers, you're making it all up," said Alicia.

"No, honestly I'm not. It's all true," said Darrell. "I saw Mr. and Mrs. Hope too, and they're seeing Sally now. They are staying the night with Miss Grayling and going back tomorrow."

"And has dear Sally found out yet whether she has a baby sister or not?" drawled Gwendoline.

Darrell felt a hot flame of temper rise up but she choked it down at once. "That's no business of yours – and it's a pity *you* didn't have about six older sisters to sit on you hard and squash you flat," said Darrell. "You'd have been a bit nicer then. But probably only a bit."

"Shhhhh! Mam'zelle coming!" hissed the girl at the door, and in came Mam'zelle, rather cross this morning because the third form had just proved extraordinarily stupid. Darrell didn't mind how cross Mam'zelle or Miss Potts were that day. She kept thinking of Sally's happiness. She wondered how she was getting on.

Sally and her mother and father were happy together. The curious wall that Sally had built up between herself and her mother had fallen away, because suddenly the jealousy was gone. Her mother had left the baby alone to come to *her* – and Sally was content. Not that she wanted Baby Daphne to be left with strangers – but it was a sign to her that her mother thought of her and loved her. Funny little Sally!

"We'll come and see you tomorrow before we go home," said her mother, when Matron said it was time for Mr. and Mrs. Hope to go. "And, if you *badly* want me to, I'll stay an extra day, and let Daddy go home without me."

"No," said Sally, with a sigh. "Don't let's leave Baby

too long! And I know Daddy would rather you went with him. I'm getting better already, Mother. I'll soon be well – and I shall feel quite different."

Then Mrs. Hope knew for certain that Sally was her own unselfish little girl again, and she was glad. What a good thing Darrell Rivers had written to her as she did! Now everything was all cleared up.

Darrell was allowed to go and see Sally twice a day, long before anyone else was. Sally welcomed her eagerly. Sally was so different now – no longer a prim, closed-up little person, but a friendly, eager girl, ready to talk about her home and her dogs and her garden, asking Darrell about the lessons and the games, if Mam'zelle was cross, and what Miss Potts said, and whether Gwendoline and Mary-Lou were still friends.

"You know, Sally," said Darrell, "when I felt so awfully frightened because I thought I'd injured you and might be sent away from here, I suddenly knew how it must feel to be like Mary-Lou – always scared of everything! And I was sorry I'd teased her so."

"Let's be nice to Mary-Lou," said Sally, who, with her strength returning to her, and with Darrell's friendly visits each day, felt that she could be nice even to Gwendoline! "Tell her I'd like her to come and see me."

Mary-Lou was overwhelmed by this message. Fancy Sally choosing *her* for one of her first visitors! Armed with a big bottle of barley-sugar she went to the San. Sally looked rather pale, but very different. Her eyes were bright, and she smiled. She welcomed Mary-Lou graciously.

They talked, and Mary-Lou blossomed a little. She was not afraid of Sally. She told her all sorts of things. Then she looked worried.

"You know, Sally, I do wish Gwendoline wouldn't keep saying horrid things about Darrell. She keeps trying to make me think that Darrell is playing nasty tricks on me. Or that Alicia is. My ink-pot was spilt yesterday all over my atlas, and Gwendoline says she's sure Darrell did it, because she saw that Darrell's fingers were all inky that day."

"As if Darrell would do anything like *that*!" said Sally, indignantly. "How *can* you listen to Gwendoline when she says things like that?"

"I can't stop her," said Mary-Lou, the scared look coming into her face again. "You see, she will keep saying that I'm her friend, and she can tell me anything."

"*Are* you her friend?" demanded Sally.

"No. Not really. But I don't like telling her I don't want to be," said Mary-Lou. "Don't call me a coward. I know I am. But I can't help it."

"Time to go, Mary-Lou," said Matron, coming in. "Tell Darrell she can come in half an hour's time, and bring a simple game with her – Happy Families or something. Not Snap."

So Darrell came, armed with Happy Families. But the two girls didn't get beyond dealing out the cards. They talked about Mary-Lou and Gwendoline.

"Gwendoline's poisonous," said Sally. "She's always talking against you and Alicia, making out you play those rotten tricks on Mary-Lou."

"I wonder who does them?" said Darrell. "One of the other Tower girls, do you think? What about Evelyn from West Tower? She's always doing silly, teasing tricks."

"No. I should think it might be Gwendoline herself!" said Sally, looking at the cards in her hand.

Darrell stared at her in surprise. "Oh, *no*," she said. "Why, Gwendoline and Mary-Lou are *friends*."

"So Gwendoline says. But Mary-Lou says different," said Sally.

"Yes, but – *no* one could be so awful as to pretend to be friends with someone and then to play rotten tricks on them all the time!" said Darrell. "It would be a disgusting thing to do."

"I think Gwendoline *is* disgusting!" said Sally. "I never could bear her. A real double-faced person, who doesn't care tuppence for anyone in the world but herself."

Darrell looked at Sally. "I think you're very clever," she said. "You seem to know all about people – much more than I do. I'm sure you know more about Mary-Lou than I do, already."

"I like Mary-Lou," said Sally. "If only we could get her to be not so scared of everything, she'd be fun."

"But how can we?" said Darrell, shuffling all the cards together absent-mindedly. "Oh, dear – look what I've done. Never mind, it's more interesting to talk than play cards just now. How *can* we cure Mary-Lou? I've tried to buck her up and make her ashamed of herself, but it doesn't seem to do any good."

"Can't you see that she *is* ashamed of herself already?" said Sally, unexpectedly. "But being ashamed doesn't give her any courage. Nobody can give her pluck except her own self."

"Well – think of a way to make her give herself pluck!" said Darrell. "I bet you can't!"

"I'll think tonight, before I go to sleep," said Sally. "And when you come and see me in the morning, I'll have a plan – you see if I haven't!"

Sally's Plan

Darrell went to see Sally at Break as usual the next morning. Sally greeted her eagerly. "Well, I've thought of something! It's not a *fright*fully good plan, but it will do as a beginning."

"What is it?" asked Darrell, thinking how pretty the

127

plain little Sally looked that morning, with colour in her cheeks, and twinkles in her eyes.

"Well, listen. What about you pretending to be in difficulties in the pool, when you get the chance, and yelling out to Mary-Lou to run and get the life-belt quickly and throw it to you?" said Sally. "If she does that, and feels that she has saved you from going under, she'll be awfully bucked. We all know how to chuck the belt into the water. It would be quite easy for her to do."

"Yes. It's a good idea," said Darrell. "I might try it out tomorrow. I'll give the tip to the others not to throw it to me, but to let Mary-Lou. At least, I'll tell the people I can trust – not dear Gwendoline, for instance! Do you really think it will help Mary-Lou not to be so scared of things if she does that?"

"Well, it seems to me that Mary-Lou will never be able to face up to things unless she thinks she's got a bit of good sense and courage in her to start with!" said Sally, seriously. "You can't possibly do anything if you *think* you can't. But you can do impossible things sometimes if you think you *can*."

"How do you know things like that?" asked Darrell, in admiration. "I wish *I* did!"

"Oh, it's not very difficult really," said Sally. "All you do is put yourself into the place of the other person, and feel like them, and then think how you could cure yourself if you were them. That sounds muddled – but I can't very well say exactly what I mean. I haven't the words."

"Oh, I know what you mean, all right!" said Darrell. "You do what Mother is always telling *me* to do – get into somebody else's skin, and feel what *they're* feeling. But I'm too impatient to do that. I'm too tightly in my *own* skin! You're not. I think you're clever and kind, Sally."

Sally went red and looked pleased. She also looked

128

rather shy. "I'm not clever – and you know I'm not kind, by the way I behaved to Daphne," she said. "But it's nice that you think so, anyway! Do you think you can work the idea out all right, Darrell?"

"Oh, yes, I think so," said Darrell. "I'll try it tomorrow, when we're in the pool. Mary-Lou has got a bit of a cold and isn't allowed to bathe this week, so she'll be watching by the side. She can easily go and get the life-belt and fling it to me. Won't she be bucked!"

"I guess she's glad she's got a cold this week," said Sally, with a chuckle. "She does so hate the water! I bet she'll never learn to swim."

"It was funny when Matron said Mary-Lou had a cold and wasn't to go in the water," said Darrell, "because dear Gwendoline immediately began to sniff like anything in class, hoping Miss Potts would report it to Matron, and *she* would be told too that she mustn't bathe. She's even worse than Mary-Lou at getting into the water!"

"What happened?" asked Sally, with interest. "Oh, I do wish I was back in school. I'd die of boredom if I hadn't got you to come and tell me things."

"Well, Miss Potts got angry with Gwendoline's sniffs and sat on her properly," said Darrell. "And then Gwendoline said she was sure she had caught Mary-Lou's cold, so Miss Potts sent her to Matron – and Matron gave her a large dose of awful medicine, and was most unsympathetic – and she didn't say Gwendoline wasn't to go into the water, she said the salt in it would probably do her good. And I heard her tell Miss Potts that the only way to take Gwendoline's tales was with a pinch of salt, so she might as well swallow some in the pool!"

Sally laughed heartily. She could just picture Gwendoline's anger at having medicine for no real reason, and not getting her way after all. Darrell got up.

"There's the bell," she said. "I'll come back after

129

lunch and tell you all the tit-bits. I haven't told you yet how Alicia and Betty tied thread to a pile of Mam'zelle's books on her desk, and Alicia pulled the thread and jerked off the books under Mam'zelle's very nose! I thought Irene would die of laughing. You know how she explodes."

"Oh, yes, do come back and tell me everything," said Sally, who looked forward to Darrell's visits more than to anything else. "I do love hearing you talk."

It was strange how completely different Sally seemed now. When Darrell looked back and remembered the quiet, self-contained, serious person Sally Hope had always appeared, it seemed impossible that she had turned into the laughing, eager, twinkling-eyed girl in the bed – a sensible, kindly girl with a real sense of fun.

"She's not such good fun as Alicia, of course," said Darrell to herself, "but she's more *trust*able, somehow. And she isn't as sharp-tongued, though she's just as clever in what she thinks about people."

Darrell carefully thought out the plan for tricking Mary-Lou into sudden good sense and a bit of pluck. It should be quite easy. She would tell Alicia and Betty to take the others to the other end of the pool, so that she, Darrell, would be alone in the deep end. Then she would struggle and yell and pretend she had cramp.

"I'll yell out to Mary-Lou and shout, 'Quick, quick, throw me the life-belt!'," she thought. "Then surely Mary-Lou will do that, and I'll clutch it and pant and puff, and call out, 'Oh, Mary-Lou, you've saved my life!' And if after that Mary-Lou doesn't have a better opinion of herself, it'll be queer. Once she knows she can really do something like that, maybe she'll pull herself together and be able to face up to some of the silly things that scare her!"

It really did seem a very good plan. Darrell let Alicia and Betty into the secret. "It's really Sally's idea," said

Darrell. "It's a very good one, don't you think so?"

"Well – why ever should you want to bother your-selves with that silly little baby of a Mary-Lou?" said Alicia in surprise. "You'll never make her any better. She's hopeless."

"But we *might* make her better," argued Darrell, rather disappointed with the way that Alicia took the idea.

"Not much chance," said Alicia. "I expect what *will* happen is that Mary-Lou will be too scared stiff to do a thing, and will simply stand blubbing by the pool and let somebody else run for the life-belt. And that will make her worse than ever, because everyone will des-pise her."

"Oh," said Darrell, feeling damped. "That would be sickening. Oh, Alicia, I didn't think of that."

Darrell told Sally what Alicia had said. "I quite see what she means," she said. "And it might make Mary-Lou worse instead of better, because everyone would laugh at her. You see, Alicia is awfully smart, Sally – never thought of that, did we?"

"Yes. Alicia *is* very smart," said Sally, slowly. "But sometimes she's a bit *too* smart, Darrell. She's forgot-ten something important."

"What's that?" asked Darrell.

"She's forgotten that it's *you* who are going to struggle and yell for help," said Sally. "Everyone knows that Mary-Lou thinks you're wonderful and would do anything in the world for you – if you'd let her. Well, here is something she *can* do – and *will* do! You see if I'm not right. Give Mary-Lou a chance, Darrell. Alicia sees her as a weak little cry-baby. But she could be something more than that, for the sake of someone she loved."

"All right, Sally. I'll give her a chance," said Darrell. "But I can't help thinking Alicia is right. She really is smart, you know, and can always size people up. I wish

131

she wasn't friends with Betty. I wish she was *my* friend!"

Sally didn't say any more. She played dominoes with Darrell and was rather quiet. Matron came and shooed Darrell away soon after that, and she had to go off to her prep.

"I'm going to try out Sally's idea on Mary-Lou," she told Alicia. "So you and Betty will take the others off to the shallow end, won't you, when you see Mary-Lou standing by the deep end? Then I'll yell out, and we'll see if Mary-Lou has the nerve to throw me the belt. It's not much to do!"

"It'll be too much for *her*," said Alicia, rather annoyed that Darrell should still think of going on with the idea after she had poured cold water on it. "Still, we'll see."

So, the next afternoon the plan was carried out. The first-formers went chattering down to the pool in their bathing costumes and beach-gowns. Gwendoline went too, looking sulky because the form had teased her unmercifully about her pretended cold!

Mary-Lou had not changed into her bathing-things, and was pleased. She did so hate the water! Darrell called to her. "You can throw pennies in for me, Mary-Lou, and watch me dive for them in the deep end!"

"All right," said Mary-Lou, pleased, and put some pennies into her pocket. Her cold was almost better. What a pity! She had so much enjoyed not having to bathe!

Into the water plunged the girls. Some jumped in, some dived in. Only Gwendoline went cautiously down the steps. But even she went in quickly for once, because somebody gave her a push and down she went, spluttering and gasping. And when she arose, angry and indignant, not a single girl was near her, of course, so she had no idea at all who had pushed her. Darrell or Alicia she supposed. Beasts!

Mary-Lou was at the deep end, watching the others.

At least, she watched Darrell mostly, admiring the way she swam, cutting the water so cleanly with her strong brown arms, and thrusting through the waves like a small torpedo. Mary-Lou put her hands into her pocket and felt the pennies there. It was nice of Darrell to ask her to throw them in for her. It was always nice to do anything for Darrell, even if it was only a little thing.

"Come down to the other end and let's have a race!" cried Alicia suddenly. "Come on, everyone."

"I'll just stay here for a bit and dive for pennies!" yelled Darrel. "I'm puffed for racing. I'll get out of your way when you start. Hie, Mary-Lou, have you got the pennies?"

Alicia and Betty, who were the only girls in the plan, watched what would happen. Both girls felt certain that Mary-Lou would weep and remain rooted to the rocks when Darrell called out. She wouldn't have the nerve to rush for the life-belt!

The other girls were splashing about, getting into position for the race. Mary-Lou threw a penny into the water and Darrell dived for it.

She brought it up in triumph. "Throw another, Mary-Lou!" she cried. Splash! In went another penny. Darrell dived again, thinking that now was the time to pretend to be in difficulties. She came up, gasping.

"Help! Help!" she cried. "I've got cramp! Quick, Mary-Lou, the life-belt, the life-belt! Help, help!"

She threw her arms about and struggled, letting herself sink under a little. Mary-Lou stared, absolutely petrified. Alicia nudged Betty.

"Just what I thought," she said in a low voice. "Too much of a ninny even to get the life-belt!"

"HELP!" yelled Darrell, and two or three of the other girls, thinking she was really in trouble, swam strongly up the pool.

But somebody else reached Darrell first! There was a resounding splash, and into the water, fully dressed,

133

Somebody helped the shivering Mary-Lou out of the pool

jumped the scared Mary-Lou, doing her best to remember the few swimming strokes she knew. She managed to reach Darrell, and put out her arms to her, to try and save her.

Darrell, popping her head out of the water for the second time, was filled with the utmost amazement to see Mary-Lou's wet head bobbing beside her! She stared as if she couldn't believe her eyes.

"Hold on to me, Darrell, hold on to me!" panted Mary-Lou. "I'll save you."

Well Done, Mary-Lou!

Then up came the other two or three swimmers and called out sharply. "What's up, Darrell? Get out of the way, Mary-Lou."

But Mary-Lou couldn't. She had made her great effort, jumped into the water and swum a few strokes – but now her strength was gone and her clothes were weighing her down. One of the swimmers took her safely to the side, where she clutched a bar, panting, looking anxiously over her shoulder to see if Darrell was safe.

She had apparently quite recovered from the cramp, for she was swimming over to Mary-Lou with strong, quick strokes, her eyes gleaming.

"Mary-Lou! You jumped right into the water, and you hardly knew how to swim! You're an idiot, but you're the pluckiest idiot ever I knew!" cried Darrell.

Somebody helped the shivering, astonished Mary-Lou out of the pool. Miss Potts came down the cliff at that moment and was amazed to see a fully-dressed and soaking Mary-Lou scrambling out, with girls crowding round her, clapping her on the shoulder and praising her.

"What's happened?" said Miss Potts, in wonder. "Did Mary-Lou fall in?"

Eager voices told her what had happened. "She jumped in to save Darrell! Darrell had the cramp and yelled for the life-belt. But Mary-Lou jumped straight in to save her – and she can hardly swim!"

Miss Potts was as astonished as everyone else. *Mary-Lou!* But Mary-Lou screamed if she saw an earwig! What an amazing thing.

"Why didn't she throw the life-belt?" asked Alicia.

"It w-w-w-wasn't there," answered Mary-Lou, her teeth chattering partly from cold and partly from excitement and shock. "It's g-g-g-gone to be m-m-m-mended. Didn't you know?"

No. Nobody had noticed that it was gone from its place. So Mary-Lou had not been stupid. She had known the life-belt was not there to save Darrell, and she had done the next best thing – jumped in herself. Well, who would have thought it?

Miss Potts hurried the shivering Mary-Lou up the cliff. Darrell turned to face Alicia, her eyes shining.

"Well – who was right? Sally or you? Why, Mary-Lou was *brave*. It isn't as if she liked the water or even knew how to swim properly! She was as brave, no, braver than any of us, because she must have been so afraid!"

Alicia could be generous even when she was proved to be in the wrong. She nodded. "Yes. She was jolly brave. I never thought she had it in her. But I bet she wouldn't have done it for anyone else but *you*!"

Darrell could hardly .wait to tell Sally. She rushed to her after tea, her face glowing. "Sally! Your idea was *mar*vellous! Simply wizard. Do you know, there wasn't a life-belt there this afternoon, so Mary-Lou jumped straight into the water with all her clothes on and everything, to try and save me!"

"Gosh!" said Sally, and her face too began to glow.

"I never thought of *that* – did you? Darrell, that's marvellous. You'll be able to tackle Mary-Lou properly now."

"What do you mean?" asked Darrell.

"Well – tell her how brave she is, and how no one ever guessed it, and now she knows it herself she'll be able to be brave about lots of other things," said Sally. "Easy! Once you can make anyone believe in themselves, they're all right."

"You *are* a funny wise person," said Darrell, admiringly. "I never think of things like that. All right. I'll do my best, and when Mary-Lou comes to see you, you tell her a few things, too!"

So Mary-Lou, to her enormous surprise and delight, became the heroine of the hour, for soon it had gone all up and down the school how she had jumped into the pool, fully-dressed, to try and save Darrell.

"It's no good you shrinking away into a corner any more, or screaming yourself blue in the face because you've seen a spider!" said Darrell. "Now we know how brave you are, we shall expect to see a bit more of your bravery!"

"Oh, *yes*," said Mary-Lou, beaming. "I'll try. Now I know I can be brave, it's different. It's when you know you can't be, that things are awful. I never, never in my life thought I would dare to jump into the deep end like that – and yet I did! I never even thought about it. I just did it. It wasn't really brave, you know because I didn't have to screw up my courage or anything."

The only person who had no word of praise for Mary-Lou was Gwendoline. For one thing she was really jealous of all the fuss made of Mary-Lou. Even the teachers made quite a to-do about it, for one and all realized that this was their one chance of making Mary-Lou realize that she *could* do things if she wanted to. Gwendoline hated all the fuss – especially as it was

Darrell that Mary-Lou had jumped in to save.

"Fancy anyone wanting to do *her* a good turn!" she thought, remembering the hard slaps she had once had from the angry girl. "I'd have left her to struggle. Stupid Mary-Lou! I suppose she will get all conceited now."

But Mary-Lou didn't. She remained her own rather shy, quiet self, but now she had more confidence, and stood up for herself better. She had been proved and had not been found wanting. She was pleased and proud, though she did not show it, as a girl like Gwendoline would have done.

For one thing she stood up to Gwendoline better, and this annoyed and exasperated Gwendoline intensely. And when Sally came back into school again, as she did in two weeks' time, she too seemed changed, and would stand no nonsense from Gwendoline. She stood up for Mary-Lou, and ticked Gwendoline off in a way that irritated her and made her long to snap at Sally.

The term went on, more and more quickly now. Only three more weeks till the holidays! Darrell could hardly believe the time had flown by so quickly.

She was working much better now, and twice she had been fifth from the top in her weekly marks. Gwendoline was the only one steadily at the bottom. Even Mary-Lou had crept up a place or two. Darrell wondered how Gwendoline was going to persuade her parents that she was top in everything at the end of the term, when she took home her report. Because her report would certainly show up Gwendoline's appalling work.

Darrell spoke to her one day about it. "Gwendoline, what will your mother and father say when they see on your report how badly you've done in your form work?" she asked, curiously.

Gwendoline looked very startled. "What do you mean – my report?" she asked.

"Golly, don't you know what reports are?" asked Darrell, in surprise. "Look, I'll show you an old one of mine. I've got my last one here, from my old school. I had to bring it with me to show Miss Potts."

She showed the report to Gwendoline who stared at it in the utmost horror. What! A list of all the subjects taken, with their marks, and position in form, and comments on the work done! Gwendoline could quite well imagine some of the comments that would be on hers!

"French. Very backward and lazy.

"Maths. Does not try in the least. Could do with some coaching in the holidays.

"Games. Disgraceful. Has no sense of sportsmanship or team-work at all."

And so on. Poor Gwendoline. It really had never occurred to her for one single moment that her bad and lazy work would be reported in this fashion to her parents. She sank down in a chair and stared at Darrell.

"But, Gwendoline, did you *never* have a report on your work before?" asked Darrell, in surprise.

"No," said the crest-fallen Gwendoline. "Never. I told you I had never been to school before I came here. Only my governess, Miss Winter, taught me – and she never made out reports, of course. She just told Mother how well I was getting on, and Mother believed her. I didn't know I was so backward till I came here."

"Well, I should think your parents will get a terrific shock when they see your report!" said Darrell, heartlessly. "I should think it will be the worst one in the school. You'll be sorry you told so many fibs to your mother and Miss Winter at half-term, when you take your report home for the holidays!"

"I shall tear it up!" said Gwendoline, fiercely, feeling that she wouldn't be able to bear the astonishment, dismay and anger of her parents when they saw her report.

"You can't," said Darrell. "It goes by post. Ha ha!

I'm jolly glad you'll be shown up at home. Mary-Lou told me some of the idiotic things you told your mother and Miss Winter at half-term. Fancy boasting like that, when you've no more brains than a mouse, and what you have you don't use!"

Gwendoline was speechless. How *dare* Darrell speak to her like that? And HOW DARE Mary-Lou repeat to the others the things she had overheard her say to her mother at half-term? Nasty, sly, disgusting little meanie! She would jolly well pay her out. She would take her fountain pen and stamp on it! She would – she would . . . Oh, there was no end to the things she would do to that beastly, ungrateful Mary-Lou!

"After I've been friends with her, too!" thought Gwendoline, angrily. "There's disloyalty for you! I hate her."

Then she began to think about her report. She felt afraid when she thought of her father reading it. That was why he had sent her away to school – because he had said she was lazy and vain and too pleased with herself. He had said some horrid things. Gwendoline tried to forget them, but they came back into her mind at odd times.

She could tell what untruths she pleased, she could boast all she liked – but if in her report there were the words "lazy, unreliable, irresponsible, conceited, stupid" – words she knew she richly deserved – well, her boasts and fibs would all be wasted.

"Only two or three weeks more," thought Gwendoline, frantically. "Can I possibly make my report any better in those few weeks? I shall *have* to try! *Why* didn't I know there were school reports before? I could have worked a bit harder. Now I shall simply have to SLAVE!"

And, to the intense astonishment of Miss Potts, and the no less intense surprise of Mam'zelle, Gwendoline began to work! How she worked! She pored over her books. She wrote endless compositions and then re-wrote them in her best writing. She was the most attentive one in the class.

"*What* has happened to Gwendoline?" asked Miss Potts of Mam'zelle. "I begin to believe she has a few – just a few – brains at last!"

"I too," said Mam'zelle. "See this French exercise? Only one mistake! Never has this happened before to Gwendoline. She is turning over a new stalk."

"New *leaf*, you mean," said Miss Potts. "Well, well, surprising things happen. There's Darrell working much better too – and Sally Hope quite a new child. And Mary-Lou has blossomed out tremendously since she jumped into the pool. But, Gwendoline is really the most surprising one. She wrote me quite a passable composition yesterday, with only six spelling mistakes. Usually she makes at least twenty. I shall be able to put '*Can* use her brains' on her report, instead of '*Never* uses her brains!' "

Gwendoline did not enjoy working so hard. Darrell laughed at her, and told the others why there was such a sudden change in the lazy Gwendoline.

"She doesn't want her people to know she told such fibs to them at half-term," she said. "Does she, Mary-Lou? That's what comes of boasting, Gwendoline. Sooner or later you have to eat your words."

Mary-Lou laughed too. She was much bolder nowadays, though only when Darrell or Sally were there. Gwendoline scowled at her. Horrid little turn-coat!

Gwendoline had her chance of paying Mary-Lou out the next day. She went into the common room when there was no one else there – and in Mary-Lou's locker was her precious fountain-pen! Gwendoline saw it at once.

"That's the end of *that*!" she said, spitefully, and threw it on the floor. She stamped on it hard, and the pen smashed, spilling ink all over the wooden floor.

It was Jean who saw the smashed pen first. She came into the common room to get a book, and stopped short when she saw the ink on the floor, and the bits and pieces of the blue pen.

"Golly!" said Jean. "Who's done that? What a mean trick!"

Emily and Katherine came in. Jean pointed to the pen. "Look," she said. "There's a nice little bit of spite for you."

"It's Mary-Lou's pen," said Katherine, in distress. "What a mess. Who *could* have smashed it? It's not an accident."

Mary-Lou came in with the quiet Violet. When she saw her pen, she stood and wailed aloud. "Oh! Who's done that? I had it for my birthday from Mother. And now it's all smashed!"

All the girls gathered round. Darrell and Sally and Irene were astonished to see such a silent circle when they came chattering in. They joined it, and were not surprised when Mary-Lou's wails broke out again.

"What will Mother say? She told me to take great care of it if I took it to school."

Alicia came whistling in, and she too was amazed to see the smashed pen, surrounded by its pool of deep violet ink. What a hateful thing to do to anyone!

"Who did it?" she demanded. "It ought to be reported to Potty. I bet it's Gwendoline – spiteful little beast."

"Where *is* Gwendoline?" asked Katherine. Nobody knew. Actually she was just outside the door, about to come in and pretend to be surprised and disgusted at the broken pen too. But, hearing the angry voices of the girls, her heart failed her. She stood hesitating and listening.

"Look here," said Alcia, "there's one certain way we can find out who did this – and we will too."

"What's that?" asked Katherine.

"Well, whoever stamped on this pen and smashed it must have got violet ink on the underneath of their shoes," said Alicia grimly.

"Oh, yes," said the others. "Of course!"

"That's clever of you, Alicia," said Katherine. "We'll examine every pair of shoes in our North Tower lockers – and when we see violet ink we shall know who did this."

"I know without looking!" said Darrell's scornful voice. "Nobody could have done it but Gwendoline. There's no one mean or spiteful enough but her!"

Gwendoline trembled with rage and fright. She took a hasty look at the underneath of her out-door shoes. Yes, they were stained with violet ink. Hastily she ran down the passage, ran into the little store-room, took up a bottle of violet ink, and raced to the cloak-room where the shoelockers were. If only she got there in time!

She did, because the others were busy clearing up the mess before going to examine the shoes. Gwendoline smeared some of the violet ink on the undersides of one of Darrell's shoes, then threw the bottle into a nearby cupboard. Then she hastily took off her own stained shoes, and stuffed them into the cupboard too. She pulled on a pair of slippers.

She ran out into the Court, and re-appeared at the door of the common room, apparently quite calm and unruffled. Oh, Gwendoline could act very well when it suited her!

"Here's Gwendoline!" cried Alicia. "Gwendoline, do you know anything about Mary-Lou's pen?"

143

"Pen? What about her pen?" asked Gwendoline, innocently.

"Someone's jumped on it and smashed it," said Sally.

"What a *beastly* thing to do!" said Gwendoline, putting on a disgusted face. "Who did it?"

"That's what *we* want to know," said Darrell, feeling infuriated with Gwendoline's smug expression. "And we're going to find out, see!"

"I hope you will," said Gwendoline. "Don't glare at me like that, Darrell. *I* haven't done it! Much more likely *you* have! I've noticed you've been jealous ever since so much fuss was made of Mary-Lou for jumping into the pool to rescue you!"

Everyone gasped. How could Gwendoline have the cheek to say a thing like that? Darrell began to boil. She felt the familiar red-hot flame rising up in her. Sally saw her face and put her hand on her arm.

"Go slow, old thing," she said, gently, and Darrell simmered down. But she almost choked in the effort not to rage back at the smiling Gwendoline.

"Gwendoline," said Katherine, keeping her eyes on the girl's face, "we think that whoever stamped on this pen must have violet ink on her shoes. So we mean to examine everyone's shoes, and we are sure we shall find the culprit in that way."

Gwendoline did not change her expression at all. "That's a very good idea!" she said, warmly. "A very good idea indeed. I wish I'd thought of it myself. It certainly *will* tell us who the hateful person is that smashed up poor Mary-Lou's pen."

Everyone was astonished to hear these words. A little doubt crept into the minds of the girls. Would Gwendoline be so pleased with the idea if she *had* smashed the pen? Perhaps she didn't do it after all?

"You can look at my shoes first of all, if you like," said Gwendoline, and she turned up first one foot and then another. There was no smear of ink on them, of course.

"We shall have to examine the shoes in the lockers too," said Katherine. "But first, will everyone please turn up their feet for us to see?"

Everyone did, but no one had inky marks. Then, in a solemn group, the first-formers set off for the cloak-room in which their shoe-lockers were kept.

Gwendoline's shoes were examined first, because Katherine, like the rest, felt that her shoes were more likely to be marked with ink than anyone else's. But they were not.

It was one of Darrell's shoes that was smeared with the bright-coloured ink! Katherine pulled it out, and then stared at it in the greatest amazement and horror. She held it out in silence to Darrell.

"It's – it's *your* shoe!" she said. "Oh, Darrell!"

Darrell stared at the inky shoes speechlessly. She looked round at the silent girls beside her. Some of them turned away their eyes. Alicia met hers with a hard look.

"Well, well, who would have guessed it was our straight-forward Darrell?" said Alicia, flippantly. "I wouldn't have thought it of you, Darrell."

She turned away with a look of disgust. Darrell caught hold of her arm.

"Alicia! You surely don't think *I* smashed the pen! I didn't, I tell you, I didn't! I would never dream of doing such a hateful thing. Oh, Alicia – how *could* you think I'd do it?"

"Well – you can't deny your shoe is inky," said Alicia. "You've got a dreadful temper, Darrell, and I've no doubt that in a fit of spite you stamped on Mary-Lou's pen. Don't ask me why! I haven't a temper like yours."

"But, Alicia – I'm not spiteful!" cried Darrell. "You

145

know I'm not. Alicia, I thought you were my friend! You and Betty always let me come with you. You can't believe a thing like this about a friend of yours."

"You're no friend of mine," said Alicia, and swung out of the room.

"There's some mistake!" said Darrell, wildly. "Oh, *don't* believe I did it, please, don't believe it!"

"*I* don't believe you did it!" said Mary-Lou, with tears running down her cheeks. She slipped her arm through Darrell's. "I know you didn't. I'll stick by you, Darrell!"

"And so will I, of course," said Sally's soft voice. "I can't believe you did it, Darrell, either."

Darrell was so glad to have two friends out of the stony-eyed girls around that she could almost have wept. Sally took her out of the cloakroom. Katherine looked round at the others. Her face was puzzled and dismayed.

"I can't believe it's Darrell either," she said. "But – I suppose – until it's proved differently we'll have to think of her as the culprit. It's a pity, because we've all liked Darrell."

"I never did," said Gwendoline's malicious voice. "I always thought she was capable of any mean trick, with that temper of hers."

"Shut up," said Jean, roughly, and Gwendoline shut up, well satisfied with what she had said and done.

Sally and Mary-Lou were good friends to Darrell then. They stuck by her, helped her, and stoutly defended her. Mary-Lou was openly defiant to Gwendoline. But it was all very unpleasant, and though no one had suggested a punishment for the smashing of the pen, it was punishment enough to have cold looks and cold voices always around.

Mary-Lou was very worried about the matter. It was all because of *her* pen that Darrell had got into this trouble. But she knew that it couldn't be Darrell. Like Sally, she had great faith in Darrell's natural honesty and kindness, and she was certain she could never do a mean trick to anyone.

Well, then, who could have done it? It must have been someone with a spite against both Mary-Lou and Darrell, and that person must be Gwendoline. Therefore, Gwendoline must have smeared Darrell's shoes with the ink!

But it also followed that Gwendoline's own shoes must have been inky too – and yet, when she showed them to the girls, they had been quite free from ink.

Mary-Lou lay in bed one night and frowned over the problem. How could it have been done? Was Gwendoline there when they had planned to examine the shoes? No, she wasn't.

But she might have been listening outside! And she would have had time to rush to the shoe-lockers, smear Darrell's shoes with ink, and take off her own, before sauntering back to the common room and joining in the conversation!

Mary-Lou sat up in excitement. She was suddenly sure that that was what had happened. She began to shake a little, as she always did when she was frightened or excited. Where could Gwendoline have hidden her shoes? Somewhere near the shoe-lockers, anyway. Would she have taken them away and hidden them in a safer place? Or might they still be there?

It was very late and very dark. Everyone had gone to bed long ago. Mary-Lou wondered if she dared to go down to the cloakroom and have a look round. She so badly wanted this hateful affair to be cleared up.

But she was so afraid of the dark! Still, she had been afraid of the water too, till she had jumped in to save Darrell. Perhaps she wouldn't be afraid of the dark either, if it was to help Darrell. She would try and see.

Mary-Lou crept out of bed. She didn't put on a dressing-gown. She simply didn't think of it. She crept down

147

the room and out of the door. Thank goodness there was a dim light shining in the passage!

Down the passage she went, to the stairs, and down the stairs to the rooms below. She made her way to the cloakrooms. Oh, dear, they were in pitch-darkness. Mary-Lou felt a cold shiver creeping down her back. She was frightened. In a moment she would scream. She knew she would!

"This is for Darrell! I'm doing something for somebody else and it's very important," she said to herself, as firmly as she could. "I shan't scream. But oh, *where's* the switch?"

She found it and pressed it down. At once the light came on and the cloakroom could be seen clearly. Mary-Lou drew a deep breath. Now it was all right. She wasn't in the dark any more. She felt very proud of herself for not screaming when she had so badly wanted to.

She looked at the lockers. That was Gwendoline's over there. She went to it and took out all the shoes. No – not one was inky. Now – where could the inky ones be hidden?

Mary-Lou crept down the stairs

Mary-Lou caught sight of the little cupboard nearby. She knew what was kept there. Old balls, an old racket or two, split gym shoes and all kinds of rubbish. Gwendoline's shoes *might* be there! She opened the cupboard door cautiously, afraid that a spider or earwig might come out.

She peered into the dusty rubbish, and poked it about with her finger. She pulled at an old racket – and something fell with a thud.

Mary-Lou wondered if the noise had awakened anyone and she held her breath, shaking. But no one seemed to have heard. She began to poke about again.

She found Gwendoline's shoes! She found the bottle of violet ink! That was what had fallen down with a thud! Mary-Lou looked at the bottle, and knew what Gwendoline had used it for. She looked at the shoes – and there, on the right-hand one was a broad violet mark!

With trembling hands Mary-Lou looked at the name inside the shoe again, just to make sure. Yes – there was the name, written in Miss Winter's small printing – Gwendoline Lacey.

"So it *was* Gwendoline! It *was*! I knew it wasn't Darrell!" thought Mary-Lou, joyfully. "I'll go straight back and wake the others. I'll tell them at once. Well – no, I won't. Perhaps Katherine would be cross if she knew I'd gone snooping round at night."

Mary-Lou took the bottle of ink, and the shoes. She clicked off the light and stood in darkness. But did she mind? Not a bit. She didn't once think of the black darkness as she sped upstairs. Her mind was full of her grand discovery. Darrell hadn't done it! Darrell hadn't done it!

Mary-Lou was awake first in the morning. She went to Katherine's bed and shook the surprised head-girl. "Wake up! I've something important to tell you! Wake all the others."

The others awoke when they heard the disturbance and sat up in bed, rubbing their eyes. Mary-Lou stood in front of the beds and waved Gwendoline's shoes dramatically.

"Look! I've found the *real* inky shoes! And I've found with them a bottle of violet ink! See? The person who really smashed my pen hid her own shoes and smeared Darrell's with this ink to make it seem as if *she'd* done it!"

"But *whose* shoes are they?" asked Katherine, in amazement. "And where did you get them?"

"I crept downstairs in the dark last night, and hunted in the cloakroom," said Mary-Lou triumphantly. Everyone gaped in surprise. Mary-Lou creeping down in the dark! Why, she was terrified of the dark, everyone knew that!

"I found the shoes and the bottle in the cupboard there," said Mary-Lou. "And shall I tell you the name written inside? No, I won't. Have a look round the room, all of you – and you'll see whose name is written in these shoes – you can tell by her face!"

It was true. Gwendoline's face was red with shame and horror. She stared at Mary-Lou in misery and anger. So she had been found out after all! *Why hadn't* she taken those shoes and the bottle and thrown them into the sea!

"It's Gwendoline!" said the girls, in hushed voices, staring at the red-faced girl in disgust and horror. And this time Gwendoline did not attempt to deny anything. She lay down in bed with her face hidden in the pillow.

Katherine examined the shoes and the bottle. Then she walked up to Darrell's bed and held out her hand.

"Darrell, I apologize to you for thinking for one moment it was you. I didn't really – but there seemed nothing else to think. I do beg your pardon."

"Oh – it's all right," said Darrell, her face radiant. "It's quite all right! I have felt pretty awful – but I did have Mary-Lou and Sally sticking up for me. Gwendoline won't have anyone!"

One by one the girls begged Darrell's pardon. Alicia was a little stiff about it, for she felt really ashamed of the hard words she had said. But then, Alicia *was* hard. She had a good many lessons to learn before she could lose her hardness and gain in sympathy and understanding of others.

"I'd like to be friends again," she said, awkwardly. "You come along with Betty and me as you did before, won't you?"

"Well," said Darrell, looking round at Sally's steadfast little face beside her, "well – I think if you don't mind, I'll stick to Sally and Mary-Lou. I wasn't always nice to them, but they did stick by me when I was in trouble – and they're my real friends now!"

"Oh!" said Mary-Lou, her face glowing. "Thank you, Darrell!"

Sally said nothing, but Darrell felt a delighted pinch just above her elbow. She turned and smiled. She felt very happy. Now everything would be all right again till the end of the term. Good!

She saw Gwendoline lying face downwards on her bed. She was crying bitterly. In the gladness of her heart Darrell could not bear to see even her enemy in misery. She went over to Gwendoline and shook her, but not unkindly.

"Gwendoline! I shan't say a word about this to any one and neither will the others if I ask them not to.

But you've got to buy Mary-Lou a lovely pen in return for the one you smashed. See?"

"Yes," said Gwendoline's muffled voice. "I will."

And that was all that anyone got out of Gwendoline. She could not say she was sorry. She could not even say a few ashamed words when she gave Mary-Lou a really magnificent fountain-pen she had bought. She was weaker than Mary-Lou ever was, for she hadn't even the strength to conquer herself.

"She'll never be any good, Katherine, will she?" said Darrell one day. Katherine smiled.

"It depends how long she stays at Malory Towers," she said. "It's queer how the longer you stay here the decenter you get. That's what my aunt told me. She came here, too, and she told me all kinds of stories about awful girls who got all right!"

"Not if they're like Gwendoline," said Darrell. "Nothing will ever alter *her*. I wish she was leaving!"

Gwendoline wished she was, too. The last two weeks of the term were not pleasant ones for her. Nobody mentioned the affair of the fountain-pen again, but everyone thought of it whenever they saw Gwendoline, and they would not look at her, or speak to her if they could help it. They were certain, too, that it was she who had played so many horrid tricks on Mary-Lou the whole of the term.

Poor Gwendoline! What with the girls' contempt, and her own feeling that she must work like a slave for the rest of the term, she did not have at all an easy time. But she was only reaping what she had sowed, so she could not grumble!

Darrell was very happy for the rest of that term. She and Sally and Mary-Lou were always together. Darrell no longer wanted Alicia's friendship. Sally was her friend now, and a very satisfying friendship it was, for Sally was even-tempered and well-balanced, and Darrell was not likely to fly into tempers with Sally around!

Exams. came and went. Darrell did very well. Sally did not do so well, partly because she had missed two or three weeks of the term, and partly because she had not been allowed to take the full work of her form after her illness.

Gwendoline came out better than anyone expected. "It just shows," said Miss Potts, rather severely, "it just shows, Gwendoline, what you can do if you try. Why you saved your efforts for the last two or three weeks of the term I can't imagine. Perhaps next term you will be obliging enough to work during the whole of the term!"

Gwendoline did not tell Miss Potts what had made her work so hard the last few weeks! She hoped fervently that Miss Potts would put a few nice things down on her report. What a horrid term it had been! She wished she wasn't coming back. Next term she must try and make the girls forget all she had done this term.

Darrell thought it had been a lovely term – except for Sally's illness and the two or three days when the girls had thought she had played that horrid trick on Mary-Lou. But Darrell didn't often think of those times. She was sunny-natured and liked to think of the nice things. She was sorry the term was coming to an end – but still, the hols. would be lovely!

Sally was going to stay with her in the holidays, and she was going to stay a week with Sally, too.

"You'll see my little sister," Darrell said. "You'll like her. She's a sport."

"And you'll see mine, too," said Sally, half-shyly. "I shall have to teach her to be a sport – like you!"

Mary-Lou wished she lived nearer either Sally or Darrell, then she might have been able to see them. Never mind, there was always next term, and the next – and the next . . . Mary-Lou had the sense to know that Sally was Darrell's real friend, and not herself – but she didn't mind. Darrell was fond of her and admired her.

That was all that mattered to loyal little Mary-Lou. How surprised her mother was going to be when she found that Mary-Lou was no longer afraid of the dark!

The last day came, with all its excitement of last-minute strapping of trunks and hunting for lost keys. The school became a perfect circus, and North, South, East, and West Tower girls became all mixed up everywhere.

"Always this last day is a madness!" panted Mam'-zelle, trying to force her way through a seething mass of excited girls. "Darrell! Sally! *Will* you please let me through? Ah, these mad English girls!"

Miss Potts, calm and efficient even in the midst of utter confusion, handed out small bags, marked children off the list when parents fetched them in cars, found lost keys and generally remained the one sane person in North Tower. Even Matron got flustered at times, and spent ages looking for a clothes' list she had carefully stuck into her belt.

The coaches came rolling up for the train-girls. "Come on, Darrell!" cried Sally. "Let's get the front seats. Where's Mary-Lou?"

"She's going by car!" called Darrell. "Hie, Mary-Lou, good-bye! Write to me and tell me all your news. Good-bye!"

"Come along, now!" cried Miss Potts, and the girls were all hustled into the coaches. "Where's Alicia? If she disappears again I shall really go mad. Alicia! Get in at once, and don't get out again. Good-bye, girls. Be good – or at least, as good as you can! And don't dare to face me next term without your health certificates!"

"Good-bye, Potty. Good-bye!" yelled the girls. "Good-bye, dear old Potty!"

"Goodness!" said Darrell, who had never heard Miss Potts called Potty to her face before. "How dare they!"

"It's the only time we do, just when we shout good-bye!" said Alicia with a grin. "She never seems to mind

155

then. Look at her grinning all over her face!"

Darrell leaned out of the coach. "Good-bye, Potty!" she yelled. "Good-bye – and good-bye Malory Towers!" she said, almost under her breath. "I'll be glad to see you again."

Good-bye! Good-bye till next time. Good-bye, Darrell and Sally and the rest. We'll meet you again soon. Good luck till then!

THE ENID BLYTON TRUST
FOR CHILDREN

Enid Blyton's books have sold millions of copies throughout the world and have delighted children of many nations. Here is a list of her books available in paperback from Dragon Books.

First Term at Malory Towers	£1.50	☐
Second Form at Malory Towers	£1.50	☐
Third Year at Malory Towers	£1.50	☐
Upper Fourth at Malory Towers	£1.50	☐
In the Fifth at Malory Towers	£1.50	☐
Last Term at Malory Towers	£1.50	☐
Malory Towers Gift Set	£5.50	☐
The Twins at St Clare's	£1.50	☐
The O'Sullivan Twins	£1.50	☐
Summer Term at St Clare's	£1.25	☐
Second Form at St Clare's	£1.50	☐
Claudine at St Clare's	£1.50	☐
Fifth Formers at St Clare's	£1.50	☐
St Clare's Gift Set	£5.50	☐
Mystery of the Banshee Towers	£1.25	☐
Mystery of the Burnt Cottage	£1.25	☐
Mystery of the Disappearing Cat	£1.25	☐
Mystery of the Hidden House	£1.50	☐
Mystery of Holly Lane	95p	☐
Mystery of the Invisible Thief	£1.25	☐
Mystery of the Missing Man	£1.25	☐
Mystery of the Missing Necklace	95p	☐
Mystery of the Pantomime Cat	95p	☐
Mystery of the Secret Room	£1.25	☐
Mystery of the Spiteful Letters	£1.25	☐
Mystery of the Strange Bundle	95p	☐
Mystery of the Strange Messages	95p	☐
Mystery of Tally-Ho Cottage	85p	☐
Mystery of the Vanished Prince	95p	☐

To order direct from the publisher just tick the titles you want and fill in the order form.

Fiction in paperback from Dragon Books

Richard Dubleman
The Adventures of Holly Hobbie   £1.25   ☐

Anne Digby
Trebizon series

First Term at Trebizon   £1.50   ☐
Second Term at Trebizon   £1.50   ☐
Summer Term at Trebizon   £1.50   ☐
Boy Trouble at Trebizon   £1.50   ☐
More Trouble at Trebizon   £1.50   ☐
The Tennis Term at Trebizon   £1.50   ☐
Summer Camp at Trebizon   £1.50   ☐
Into the Fourth at Trebizon   £1.25   ☐
The Hockey Term at Trebizon   £1.50   ☐
The Big Swim of the Summer   60p   ☐
A Horse Called September   £1.50   ☐
Me, Jill Robinson and the Television Quiz   £1.25   ☐
Me, Jill Robinson and the Seaside Mystery   £1.25   ☐
Me, Jill Robinson and the Christmas Pantomime   £1.25   ☐
Me, Jill Robinson and the School Camp Adventure   £1.25   ☐

Elyne Mitchell
Silver Brumby's Kingdom   85p   ☐
Silver Brumbies of the South   95p   ☐
Silver Brumby   85p   ☐
Silver Brumby's Daughter   85p   ☐
Silver Brumby Whirlwind   50p   ☐

Mary O'Hara
My Friend Flicka Part One   85p   ☐
My Friend Flicka Part Two   60p   ☐

To order direct from the publisher just tick the titles you want
and fill in the order form.

All these books are available at your local bookshop or newsagent, or can be ordered direct from the publisher.

To order direct from the publishers just tick the titles you want and fill in the form below.

Name _____

Address _____

Send to:
Dragon Cash Sales
PO Box 11, Falmouth, Cornwall TR10 9EN.

Please enclose remittance to the value of the cover price plus:

UK 45p for the first book, 20p for the second book plus 14p per copy for each additional book ordered to a maximum charge of £1.63.

BFPO and Eire 45p for the first book, 20p for the second book plus 14p per copy for the next 7 books, thereafter 8p per book.

Overseas 75p for the first book and 21p for each additional book.

Dragon Books reserve the right to show new retail prices on covers, which may differ from those previously advertised in the text or elsewhere.